"I don't know what happened between you, but I know she loved you very much."

The happy images blurred as tears filled her eyes. Was it true? Did the mother she'd always thought indifferent really love her?

A tear slid down her cheek, followed quickly by another. Kelli couldn't bear to put the pictures down long enough to wipe them away, so she let them go.

Oh, Mom! Why didn't we fix this before it was too late?

Or was it too late? Would this crazy condition of Lillian's trust help her to finally understand what had gone wrong between them?

Jason put an arm around her shoulders and squeezed. She found his silent embrace oddly comforting, and leaned into his warmth.

Still clutching the photographs, she lifted her face to look up at Jason. "I've changed my mind. I'm staying."

The Zookeeper's Daughter

VIRGINIA SMITH

THE ZOOKEEPER'S DAUGHTER

For my daughter, Christy Delliskave, who loves zoos and zoo animals as much as I do.

A Note from Ginny

My first trip to the zoo was with my grandfather way back when I was eight. I fell in love with exotic animals, and from that moment I've harbored a secret desire to work in a zoo. Life led me in a different direction; I went to work in the corporate world instead, which, at times, is pretty similar.

When I first got the idea to write a book set in a zoo, I was able to fulfill that lifelong dream. I contacted Utah's Hogle Zoo in Salt Lake City and signed up for their "Zookeeper for a Day" program. What an incredible experience! The zookeeper to whom I was assigned, Celeste, introduced me to the challenging and rewarding work of a keeper, and allowed me to help her care for a delightful assortment of animals. (Who knew porcupines could be so charming?) Then I spent several hours with Stephanie, the keeper in charge of the cats. She answered all my questions about lions and even gave me some ideas for the book. I'm more grateful to both these ladies than I can say. Utah's Hogle Zoo is bigger and far more impressive than my fictitious Cougar Bay, but I've tried to capture their dedication and enthusiasm in the pages of *The Zookeeper's Daughter*.

This book was first published under the title A Daughter's Legacy, but in my mind it has always been The Zookeeper's Daughter. I'm happy to be able to give this story its proper title and a new cover. I hope you enjoy it!

Chapter One

Of all the ways she could have chosen to spend a Thursday morning, attending a stranger's memorial service wasn't at the top of Kelli Jackson's list.

Especially when that stranger was her own mother.

Kelli faced the front of the open-air amphitheater clasping a completely dry tissue in her lap and trying to ignore the curious glances being cast her way. Apparently, everybody wanted to get a glimpse of the outsider who claimed to be Lillian Mitchell's daughter. As people filed toward their seats among the rows of semicircular wooden benches in the moments before the service began, more than one puzzled whisper reached her ears.

"I never knew Lillian had any family. Did you?"

"Can't say as I did. Looks like her, though. Wonder why Lil never talked about her."

Kelli kept her face schooled in the detached, professional mask she wore when preparing a tax return for a new client. Wouldn't do to show dismay at the humiliating affirmation that her mother hadn't even cared enough to mention to those she worked with that she'd given birth to a daughter twenty-six years before. As person after person stepped up to the podium on the center of the stage to recall incidents from Lillian's life, Kelli's gaze kept stealing to the table where the polished wooden box holding her mother's ashes rested, a single vase of flowers beside it.

The deep roar of a lion exploded in the distance, and a wave of gooseflesh rose along Kelli's bare arms as the primeval cry reverberated in the air around her. The sound echoed across the years from childhood nightmares she'd thought safely forgotten long ago.

What am I doing here, Lord? This is no place for me.

The man standing behind the podium paused in his tribute and raised his head to listen until the roar died away. His smile swept the crowded amphitheater.

"Apparently Samson would like to speak a few words on Lillian's behalf. He always was an attention hog."

The crowd's chuckle held an indulgent tone. Obviously Samson was a favorite among the mourners. Kelli shifted on the rough wooden bench.

"Actually, it's fitting that Samson be included in this service to honor Lillian. She dedicated her life to making sure that he and the rest of the animals here at Cougar Bay Zoological Park receive nothing but excellent care and the highest quality of life."

Of course she did. Kelli's lips tightened, despite her efforts to keep her expression impassive. *She cared more for those zoo animals than she did her own child.*

Which was one reason she wanted to get this ordeal over with as quickly as possible and get out of here. Back home in Denver, life could return to normal. She could go to work and lose herself in the comfort of her clients' finances. All the questions she encountered there were easy ones, with concrete answers, like, "Can I deduct the clown I hired for my daughter's birthday since I invited my boss to the party?" ("Uh, no, Mr. Farmer, I'm sorry but that's not a legitimate deduction.")

"The first time I laid eyes on Lil, she was cleaning out the chimp house." The man eulogizing Lillian—Kelli couldn't think of her as *Mom*—smiled, and from her vantage point on the first row Kelli recognized genuine affection in his face. Tall and fit, with sun-kissed brown hair curling around the collar of the tan shirt with the zoo's logo over the breast pocket. Nice looking, probably only a few years older than Kelli. What was he to Lillian? An employee, no doubt, since Lillian ran everything here at the zoo.

"I shouted through the bars that I was there to interview for the keeper position. She let me in, handed me a hose, and told me to show her my stuff." An appealing grin twisted his lips. "I must have looked hesitant, because she barked, 'You're not afraid of a little poop, are you?'"

Everyone around Kelli laughed. She couldn't hold back a smile herself. Judging from the voice she'd heard over the phone during their stilted, twice-yearly conversations, the guy had Lillian's gravelly, no-nonsense bark down pat. He must have known her pretty well, then. Kelli cast a quick glance over her shoulder at the sparsely filled benches. No doubt these people knew Lillian better than her own daughter did. How sad was that?

"I didn't bother to point out that she was wearing rubber boots, while I was in a suit and had just polished my shoes. Knowing Lil as I do now, she wouldn't have cared. It's a good thing I took the hose and got to work." His head dropped forward, and when he continued, his voice sounded choked. "Landing this job six years ago was the best thing that ever happened to me. It gave me the chance to work with someone whose devotion to animals went far beyond anyone I'd ever met, or likely will again. Lil changed my outlook on my job, and on my life. I'll never forget her."

A hushed murmur of agreement rose from the mourners as he left the stage to return to his seat on the front row, a few feet away from Kelli. She watched him covertly as the minister stepped up to the podium for his final remarks. The guy sat with his head drooping forward, hands dangling between his knees. When he brushed tears from his eyes, Kelli experienced a twinge of self-reproach.

What's wrong with me, God? My mother is dead. Why can't I grieve, like this guy?

But Kelli's soul felt leaden, numb, as the minister led them in a closing prayer. How could she grieve the loss of her mother today, when the real loss had taken place years before?

Twin tears pooled in the corners of his eyes. Jason brushed them away. Becoming emotional today surprised him. He'd already cried for Lil in the privacy of his apartment. In fact, he'd shed almost as many tears for her as he had when Dad died a few months ago. Lil would have been the first to tell him to pull himself together and get over it. He could almost hear her lecturing inside his head.

"Enough, already! There's work to do. Get over there and check that fence around the wolves' yard. If Bob gets out again we'll have AZA inspectors crawling all over the place."

A smile tugged at his mouth. Lil probably would have hated the idea of this memorial service, anyway. She wasn't one to tolerate emotional displays, said they wasted energy that should be spent accomplishing something.

Was her daughter anything like her?

Jason stole a sideways glance at the young woman whose face, though pale, bore a strong resemblance to her mother's. Same chiseled nose, same wide-set, round eyes. Although now that he took a closer look, he realized the daughter was far prettier than her mother. She was more delicate, her lips fuller and softer. And shiny with lip gloss. He'd never seen Lil wear makeup once in all the years he'd known her. Plus, this girl's thick, dark curls hung in waves down her back, while Lil had always hacked off her straight, steel-gray hair at the chin line. So maybe their features weren't so much alike after all, even though the daughter's aloof expression was a duplicate of her mother's.

Kelli. Lil told him her name was Kelli.

Did she have any idea of the blow she was about to suffer?

As though she sensed his thoughts, Kelli's head turned and she glanced his way. For the briefest of moments, clear gray eyes looked into his, and air froze in his lungs. Guilt stabbed him in the gut. He straightened quickly and focused his attention on the minister behind the podium.

Why me, Lil? I don't know if I can do it. Even for you.

Chapter Two

"I don't know what the house is like yet, Nana. I came straight to the zoo from the airport for the service."

Kelli spoke quietly into her cell phone as the mourners, most of them zoo employees judging by their clothing, filed past. She stood on a concrete path just beyond the amphitheater exit. The patchy shade from a stand of tall, skimpy trees provided scant relief from the hot Florida sun. She avoided looking anyone in the eye. No doubt she was being rude, but she didn't think she could handle their curious gazes as they mumbled platitudes about her mother.

"How was it?" Nana's voice wavered with age. "Were there a lot of people?"

"Around thirty. Everyone said nice things about her, told funny stories and all that."

"That would have been nice to hear." Nana paused. "Are you okay, sweetie?"

A drop of sweat slid between her shoulder blades. Kelli held the phone with one hand and mopped at her damp forehead with the tissue. "I'm okay. It's really humid here, though. And hot. It's only ten o'clock in the morning and it must be ninety degrees already."

Kelli folded the tissue and scrubbed the back of her neck beneath her heavy mane of hair as the stream of people leaving the service slowed to a trickle. She spotted the last two men hovering just inside the shoulder-high hedge that surrounded the amphitheater, both of them looking her way. One was Lillian's attorney, who'd met Kelli at the zoo entrance and brought her inside for the service. The other was the guy who'd spoken last and sat near her. They were obviously waiting for her to finish her conversation.

"Nana, I have to go. I need to talk to the lawyer."

"All right. Call me tonight."

"I will. Love you."

"Love you, too, sweetie."

Kelli disconnected the call and slipped the phone into her purse. When she did, the men stepped through the exit and headed toward her. Mr. Lewis carried the vase of flowers in one hand and his briefcase in the other, and the younger man held—

Her breath caught at the sight of the polished wooden box in his hands.

The serious-faced attorney stepped into the small patch of shade. "Ms. Jackson, allow me to introduce Jason Andover, an employee of your mother's."

Jason shifted the box to the crook of his left arm and extended his right. "Ms. Jackson."

"Please call me Kelli." His hand felt cool and dry next to her damp palm. Now that she could see him face-to-face, she felt a little flustered. He was quite handsome, with a golden tan and green-brown eyes that seemed to pierce straight into hers.

"Kelli." He drew out her name, making the most of both syllables in a faint southern drawl that sent a tickle through her insides. "I'm sorry for your loss. Lil was a good boss, a good woman. She meant a lot to all of us here at the zoo. She was almost like a mother to me."

The words hit her like a slap. Almost like a *mother*? How *nice* for them both. Kelli tried to hold her bitterness at bay, but when his eyes narrowed almost imperceptibly, she realized her lips were pressed tightly together.

"Thank you," she managed as she extracted her hand from his grip. "And thank you for your kind words during the service. I'm sure my—mother would have appreciated them." She turned to Mr. Lewis. "I'd like to get started going through her house. Do you have the key?"

To her surprise, Jason answered. "It's in the office. Follow me." He turned abruptly and strode away, not bothering to check to see if she followed.

Odd. What was he upset about? She was the one whose mother apparently mothered everyone but her own daughter. She raised her eyebrows in a silent question to the attorney, but he merely nodded for her to follow Jason's retreating back. With a sigh, Kelli hitched her purse strap higher on her shoulder and trailed after him down the sidewalk beside a high hedge with lush pink blossoms.

Mr. Lewis fell into step beside her. "There are a couple of things we need to go over."

"You mean her will?"

He nodded and lifted his briefcase slightly. "I have everything with me. Do you feel up to talking now, before you go to the house?"

Kelli looked sideways at him, discomfort tickling in the pit of her stomach when he didn't meet her eye. Had Lillian left a pile of debt for her daughter to settle? A financial tangle that would take months to unravel? Well, hopefully the house would sell quickly, and at a price high enough to take care of the balance of the mortgage with enough left over to resolve the rest. There would probably be some large medical bills. Kelli's stomach churned with an unnamed emotion. Did her mother even have medical insurance?

What kind of daughter doesn't know things like that?

They passed a large, dome-shaped cage full of medium-size brown monkeys with long tails. One let out a loud screech that made her jump. As the sound continued and gained in volume, she clapped hands to her ears. "What in the world?"

Ahead on the path, Jason glanced backward. "Howler," he said over his shoulder.

"No kidding." Kelli eyed the bearded primate, whose head turned as she passed, liquid brown eyes fixed on her face. The creature watched her with human-like intensity, but the smell emanating from the exhibit—or maybe from the howlers them-selves—was pure animal, and seemed to be magnified by the heat. She wrinkled her nose and breathed through her mouth until they were downwind.

The path wound through a smaller set of cages containing a variety of large, colorful birds. A macaw combed its wing with a hooked beak as they passed, and Kelli admired the way the sun turned the feathers fiery red. Now, birds like these she could handle. Just as long as she stayed away from the lions.

She suppressed a shudder.

Finally, they arrived at the office, a smallish one-story build-ing tucked behind the ticket booth where they'd stashed her lug-gage when she arrived by taxi from the airport. Jason politely held open the door as she entered.

Kelli blinked in the cool interior to clear her sun-dazzled eyes. Four office desks were crowded into this room, three of them occupied. As Jason led them toward a door in the back wall, one of the girls, a blonde who Kelli vaguely recognized from the memorial service, stood and stepped in front of her.

"Hi, I'm Angela. I just want to tell you how sorry we all are."

Kelli shook her hand. "Thank you."

"If there's anything we can do," the girl's gesture included the others in the room, "don't hesitate to ask."

What that would be, Kelli couldn't imagine, but she nodded. "I appreciate that."

The back office was barely big enough for the three of them. A cluttered desk dominated the room, with two hard plastic chairs in front of it. On one corner an engraved name-plate read *Lillian Mitchell, Director.* The walls were cluttered with unframed pictures of animals held in place with thumb-tacks, alongside crayon drawings with notations like, "Thank you for shoing me the munkes," and beneath a gray drawing that vaguely resembled an elephant, "Elsie is my favrit." Kelli noticed that someone had brought her luggage in here and piled it in the corner.

Jason set the box containing Lillian's ashes on top of a crowded bookcase. He started to round the desk toward the pad-ded desk chair, then hesitated. With a gesture for Kelli to take that place, he waited for her to be seated before settling his large frame on a plastic chair.

Why was he being included in this conversation? Had Lillian named him in her will? Probably, because he said she'd been like a mother to him. Kelli kept a smile fixed on her lips in spite of the bitter taste on the back of her tongue. She felt entirely out of her element here, like she didn't belong.

Which, of course, I don't.

Mr. Lewis set his briefcase on top of a pile of papers on the surface of the desk and clicked open the latches. "As you probably know, your mother made plans to settle her estate six months ago, shortly after she was diagnosed with cancer."

Kelli swallowed, her throat dry. The truth was, she didn't know Lillian was ill until three days ago, when the hospital called to inform her that her mother had died. Six months? She'd found out she had cancer last January, then.

Why didn't she tell me?

"No, I wasn't aware of that."

Jason's head jerked up, his eyes narrowing into a speculative stare. Heat flared into Kelli's face. What reason did he have to look at her with that judgmental expression? Who was this guy, anyway? Whoever he was, she didn't like him. No matter how handsome he was, he had no right to look at her like she had done something wrong. It wasn't her fault Lillian had chosen to keep her illness from her daughter. Kelli refused to return his gaze, but looked pointedly at Mr. Lewis.

The attorney cleared his throat and extracted a document from the case. "I've known Lil for more than ten years, since I was first invited to serve on the zoo's board of directors. I'd never handled any personal business for her until she asked me to set up her trust, in which—"

"A trust?" Kelli couldn't filter the surprise out of her voice.

"Yes. Are you familiar with the purposes of a trust?"

She nodded. "I'm an accountant, so I'm quite familiar with them. A person transfers all assets into the trust to avoid probate when he or she dies. But it's usually only necessary if the assets exceed $500,000, or if there are minor children to be cared for." Surely Lillian's estate didn't come close to that amount. And at twenty-six years old, Kelli could hardly be considered a minor.

"Usually. In this case, Lillian chose a testamentary trust so she could specify certain—" he appeared to search for a word "—conditions related to the disbursement of her estate."

She couldn't stop herself from glancing at Jason. The guy watched her with an intensely speculative gaze that unnerved her. She looked quickly away.

Lillian, what have you done?

With iron control, Kelli managed to keep her tone even. "Go on, please."

Mr. Lewis handed her the thick stack of papers, held together with a large paper clip. "With the exception of a few minor bequeaths, your mother named you and Cougar Bay Zoological

Park as equal beneficiaries in the trust. The zoo's half is to be paid out immediately after her affairs have been settled, and the liquid assets will go into the fund for the new African Lion Habitat. Yours will be distributed after six months, provided the conditions of the trust are met."

A lion habitat. Terrific. Of all the things Lillian could have done with her money, that was the one sure to cause the most agony for her only daughter. No wonder she chose not to mention it to Kelli.

She sat taller in the chair, her spine rigid. She would not react to this, not in front of strangers. Especially not in front of Jason, who sat there purposefully trying to unnerve her with his silence and his narrow-eyed stare. "And what are the conditions of the trust?"

"That you accept employment as a keeper at Cougar Bay Zoological Park for a period of six months. At the end of that time your work will be evaluated by your supervisor, the new zoo director, and if all is satisfactory, you'll receive your half of the assets in the trust."

A blast of laughter escaped Kelli's mouth before she could stop it. "Me, work in a zoo? That's ridiculous." She leaned forward across the desk. "I don't like animals. My mother knew that."

Mr. Lewis had the grace to look embarrassed. He handed her a sealed envelope. "Perhaps she explained her reasons here. I was instructed to give this to you after she passed."

Kelli took the envelope and noted her name scrawled across the front in Lillian's handwriting. She tossed it and the trust document on the desk. There was no explanation that could possibly explain this—this outrageous condition.

"I won't do it," she said.

Mr. Lewis cleared his throat again. "Before you say that, you might want to know the value of Lil's estate."

Kelli's head shot up. "I don't care how much it is. There isn't possibly enough money in that trust to make me work in a zoo." Besides, surely Kelli would have known if Lillian was wealthy, regardless of their distant relationship.

Curiosity flickered briefly across the attorney's face, but in the next instant he was all business. "She maintained a large life insurance policy, and she carried mortgage insurance on her home, which has risen rather dramatically in value in the fifteen years since she bought it. Plus she owned twenty-five acres adjoining the zoo on the south side." Mr. Lewis's voice became soft, almost apologetic. "Between those and her IRAs, the value of the trust is just over $1.4 million."

The silence in the office grew heavy. The only sound was cool air blowing through a vent in the ceiling with an audible whisper. Kelli leaned slowly against the chair back. Half of $1.4 million was—she gulped—$700,000. Of course she would never wish to profit from her mother's death, but with that kind of money, she could open her own accounting firm, like she'd always wanted. And she could hire someone to help care for Nana, who was growing frighteningly frail as her eighty-second birthday approached. They wouldn't have to face the looming specter of a nursing home.

But could Kelli handle working *in a zoo* for six months, even for Nana?

She stole a glance at Jason. He sat unnaturally still, his muscular shoulders rigid, tense. Those green-brown eyes watched her closely. A horrible suspicion stole over her.

Her gaze slid back to Mr. Lewis. "You said the zoo director would evaluate my performance at the end of six months. Has the zoo named a replacement for my mother?"

"Not yet, but the board will confirm the appointment within a few days. That was a condition of the zoo receiving its half of the estate." Mr. Lewis glanced at the younger man seated beside him. "The new zoo director will be Jason Andover."

Chapter Three

*B*eneath the cover of the desk, Kelli's nails dug into the fleshy part of her palms. The sharp pain helped her maintain a composed expression. At least, she hoped so. She could not force herself to look at Jason.

How had he managed to convince Lillian to agree to this ridiculous condition? No doubt he'd charmed her with his good looks and that oh-so-subtle southern accent. In her job at the accounting firm, Kelli had seen several older women fall victim to an attractive younger man with dishonorable intentions. She'd never thought of Lillian being susceptible in that way, though. Which proved once again how little Kelli had known her own mother.

I should have been here for her. Then she wouldn't have gone looking for a replacement for her affections.

Both men were waiting for her to say something, but her whirling thoughts made an intelligent reply impossible. She needed to get away to think, to pray.

Mr. Lewis rescued them from the awkward silence.

"I expect you'll want to read through the trust document before you make your decision. Lil did include a provision for you in case you decided not to accept her conditions." He extracted another envelope from his briefcase and handed it to Jason. "She also asked me to deliver this."

Jason hesitated, then took the letter almost reluctantly. He folded the envelope and shoved it into his breast pocket. She narrowed her eyes. What had been her mother's parting words to this—this gold-digger?

On second thought, she didn't want to know.

She pushed the chair back from the desk and addressed Mr. Lewis. "If you don't mind, I'd like to see the house now. Do I need to call a taxi, or can you run me over?"

"You don't need a taxi." He closed the case and snapped the clasps shut. "Lil's house is here, at the back of the zoo."

Kelli's jaw went slack. "She lived at the zoo?"

Jason answered. "Not at the zoo. Her house is just beyond the rear wall. I'll take you."

Terrific. She'd rather not spend any more time in his company than necessary, but Mr. Lewis wasn't jumping in with an offer.

"Thank you." At least her voice sounded cordial, even though she still couldn't bring herself to look at the man.

He rose and came around the desk to slide open the center drawer. Kelli rolled the chair as far back as the limited space allowed, but she was still close enough that his thigh brushed her arm. She jerked away, her skin tingling, and tried to ignore the masculine scent that clung to him. No hint of cologne, just the clean smell of soap, or maybe shampoo.

From the drawer he retrieved a set of keys, which he handed to her. "House and car. She told me there's an extra set of each in her home office."

She took them without a word and gathered the trust document and letter Mr. Lewis had given her.

The attorney stood when she did, and extended a business card. "If you have any questions, don't hesitate to call."

Several pressed on her mind and she hadn't even read the documents yet. But he probably couldn't tell her why her mother did this bizarre thing. Hopefully, the letter would give a satisfactory answer. She pulled out one of her own cards to give to the attorney. On an impulse, she extracted a second card and handed it to Jason. As Lilian's successor, he might need to get in touch with her if he came across anything personal in the files.

Jason pocketed the card without looking at it. When she started to pick up her suitcase, Jason leaned forward to grab it, along with the polished box containing her mother's remains.

"Let me get that for you. It's a bit of a hike to the back."

The case had wheels, but rather than argue she inclined her head. "Thank you." He was polite, she'd give him that.

Shouldering her laptop case, she preceded the men through the door. Everyone but Angela had left the office, and the blonde sat behind her desk, a phone pressed to her ear. She smiled and gave Kelli a silent wave.

The Florida heat slapped at her the moment she stepped outside, the humid air heavy in her lungs. Mr. Lewis shook her hand and mumbled, "I'm sorry for your loss," before disappearing in the direction of the front gate. She watched him go through the turnstile exit as a pair of young mothers, each with a stroller and a toddler clutched by the hand, entered.

Reluctantly, she turned toward her guide.

"Lil's house is this way." Jason nodded down the path they'd taken earlier from the amphitheater.

Kelli fell in beside him. At least he didn't try to talk with her as they walked. Nor did he roll her suitcase, but carried it easily by the handle, although she knew how heavy it was. The muscles in his arm looked firm, not at all strained by the effort. Lillian's ashes were tucked snugly in the crook of his other arm. She couldn't help glancing at his profile. Under close inspection, it was hard to picture him as one of those ruthless men who preyed on lonely women. He was definitely handsome enough, but she'd always figured men like that were smooth, polished. Maybe even a little greasy. Jason's wholesome good looks didn't fall into that category.

You can't judge a book by its cover, Nana always said. Cliché, but true, and worth keeping in mind.

Thursday seemed to be a popular day at the zoo for moms with preschoolers. Small children flocked around every animal exhibit they passed, their watchful mothers hovering nearby. That was something she'd never enjoyed, though Nana had more than made up for her mother's lack of attention. Kelli dodged a pair of giggling girls who raced down the path toward a colorful peacock strutting around a grassy alcove. She caught an indulgent smile on Jason's face as the bird leaped gracefully to the top of a thick hedge, neatly avoiding his would-be admirers.

He led her around a concrete building with a sign proclaiming it to be the Small Animal House, then beside an open fenced area containing a pair of kangaroos. As they passed, one of the creatures hopped across a strip of dusty ground toward a second kangaroo snoozing on a shady patch of grass.

Their path ended at a tall wooden fence with narrow, painted slats displaying the sign, Employees Only. Jason unlocked a padlock, then gestured for her to go through. Kelli stepped into a sort of alley that ran the entire length of the zoo. On the zoo side, the fence was wooden with barbed wire at the top. Six feet inside that stood a chain-link barrier, also topped with an intimidating mass of barbed wire. A single-lane paved road ran between it and a normal-looking privacy fence, this one apparently marking the outside boundary of the zoo's property. The surface was unbroken but for a single gate.

It was to this gate Jason led her. On the other side, she stepped into a small, enclosed yard with a steep slant. A neglected-looking orange tree in one corner provided the only shade. Dry, patchy grass was strewn with weeds and needed trimming. The house, perched at the top of the hill that comprised the yard, appeared to be in decent shape, at least from the outside. She followed Jason up the slope and into a screened-in patio with a white plastic table and a single chair that both looked as though they could use a good cleaning. Using his own keys he unlocked the back door and swung it open for her.

Kelli couldn't maintain her silence any longer. "You have a key to my mother's house?" Her voice rang with disapproval.

His eyelids narrowed, and he met her gaze without flinching. "I've been feeding her cat since she went to the hospital."

"Oh." Kelli dropped her head and slipped past him into the house. Lillian had a cat? She'd never mentioned it. Another thing her only daughter should have known.

The room in which she found herself was sparsely furnished, and immaculately clean. A squarish sofa rested against the back wall to the right of the front door and beneath a wide picture window with thick tan curtains. Beside it, a wing chair sat at a ninety-degree angle facing a small television screen on top of a spindly cart that looked like it should hold a microwave oven instead. A curved laminate countertop separated the living room from a compact but fully appointed kitchen, and that was where Jason set the box.

He strode past her and placed her suitcase beside a doorway to the right. "This is the bedroom, and over there—" he pointed to a short hallway at the other end of the great room "—is her office. I've only glanced in, but I'm afraid you might have a mess to deal with. It looks about like her zoo office."

Kelli's gaze took in the room in which they stood. "This room is so clean."

"I don't think she spent much time in here." An indulgent grin twisted his lips. "She was kind of a workaholic."

He didn't *think*. Did that mean he didn't *know*, because he didn't spend any time here either? The hint of a dimple in his chin became more noticeable when his smile cocked sideways. Looking at it, Kelli found herself hoping she was wrong about him. Maybe he was nothing more than what he appeared, a nice guy who shared Lillian's love of zoo animals.

But what about that trust? How did he manage to get Lillian to name him as her successor at the zoo, and my boss?

A large yellow cat appeared from the bedroom behind him. It arched its back as it rubbed against Jason's leg, meowing loudly. The sound cut off abruptly when the animal noticed Kelli. In an instant, it shot back into the bedroom.

Jason's smile became apologetic. "Leo's a little shy around strangers, but he'll get used to you." He paused and looked away. "That is, if you're here long enough."

He's hoping I'll leave. Kelli tightened her lips at the realization. *If I walk out, what happens to my share of the trust? Does he get it, maybe?*

The question that had hovered in her mind since Mr. Lewis told her the condition of the trust shot out of her mouth before she could reconsider asking. "Tell me something. Exactly what was your relationship with my mother?"

"My rela—" Confusion slowly drained from his face as he picked up the meaning behind her question. A flush colored the already-tanned cheeks. "She was my boss. And I like to think she counted me as a friend, too. She didn't have many friends." His eyes narrowed. "Or family, either, apparently."

A jab at her. Okay, she probably deserved that. And it was certainly true. She hadn't been a model daughter. She closed her eyes and rubbed them with a thumb and forefinger. It galled her to realize Jason knew more about her mother than she did. But that didn't mean she had to be rude.

"I'm sorry. I'm not thinking very clearly right now." She opened her eyes and forced a quick smile. "Today has been a shock, to say the least."

His expression remained guarded as he stared at her. Then he nodded slowly. "I'm sure it has. I'll leave you alone." He pulled the key ring out of his pocket. When he had twisted off a key, he placed it on the empty countertop. "Now you have all the house keys."

A glimmer of light caught his eyes and warmed his gaze. Kelli found herself wanting to return his smile.

Instead, she looked down at the beige carpet between them. "Thank you."

"If you need anything, call the zoo office and ask for me."

He hesitated as though he wanted to add something, but then changed his mind and left. Kelli crossed to the back door and lifted one of the mini blinds' slats to watch as he strode across the weedy yard. When he'd disappeared through the back fence, she turned and leaned against the door. The room was sterile, eerily so.

She looked at the box. Its presence seemed to dominate the silent house. Here she was, alone at last with her mother.

"Lillian, why did you do this? Are you trying to punish me?"

Her questions fell flat. The polished wood swam in Kelli's vision when the first tears since that terrible phone call three days ago filled her eyes. Impatiently, she brushed them away, much like she'd seen Jason do during the service. With a loud sigh, uttered more for its noise value than anything else, she lifted her laptop case to the counter and opened the front flap, where she'd placed her copy of the trust and her mother's letter. Maybe she'd find some answers there.

Jason let himself through the gate and paused on the other side, his breath whooshing out as his lungs deflated. That girl was more like Lil than he'd originally thought. The direct way she had of fixing those gray eyes on him, of thrusting out her chin like she was ready to take on anyone who stood in her way. Just like Lil used to do when they were working on a problem with one of the animals. Only he'd caught a couple of emotions flickering across Kelli's face that he'd never seen Lil display. Right before he left, for instance, she'd looked so tired, even a little vulnerable. Small. Lil was always larger than life, in control—of her emotions and of any situation that arose.

"Oh, Lil, we're sure going to miss you around here."

He crossed the trail to lean on the top rail of the fence surrounding Cali and Halil's yard, and watched the kangaroos snooze in the shade. They'd been at Cougar Bay for a couple of years, compliments of a failed private zoo up in Kentucky. Lil had been ruthless in her determination to acquire them, their first large marsupials. They'd quickly become a favorite among zoo guests.

What had happened between Lil and her daughter? Jason's conversations with his boss in the past few weeks had been frustratingly unenlightening. He hadn't known what to expect from Kelli, but in some part of his mind he thought she'd be Lil's total opposite. Flighty, maybe. Or perhaps openly rebellious, with purple hair or pierced eyebrows or something. What else besides rebellion could drive such a wedge between a mother and daughter? He certainly hadn't expected an intelligent, beautiful woman with pain lurking in her eyes.

But he probably should have. Lil's words, uttered in a raspy, shallow voice in her hospital bed the day before she died, rang in his memory.

"She won't be happy about this, Jason. With good reason. It's going to be painful, and she'll probably hate you." She'd paused to catch her breath. "Don't go easy on her, though. Everybody needs to face their fears. And if she fails…" Lil's voice had trailed off.

Jason heaved a sigh. He was getting accustomed to being hated by beautiful women. But after meeting Kelli Jackson, he found himself waging a private battle. On the one hand, his loyalty was to the animals of Cougar Bay Zoological Park, who depended on him for their very existence. That's why Lil had trusted him to replace her as zoo director.

On the other hand, he'd only met her daughter an hour before, but he knew one thing: he didn't want to see Kelli fail.

Chapter Four

The wing chair faced the tiny television screen, and from the slightly worn appearance of the armrests, Kelli assumed that was Lillian's habitual seat. She settled on the cushion on the opposite end of the sofa and slid off her shoes before tucking her feet beneath her. Her name, scrawled in Lillian's untidy handwriting, drew her attention to the letter. She freed it from the paperclip and stared at it for a long moment. Lillian had rarely written to her over the years, and when she did, it was always a quick note inside a card on her birthday or at Christmas. Or brief, cryptic e-mails. Kelli couldn't remember receiving an actual letter since she went to live with Nana when she was eight. She set the envelope on the cushion beside her. Easier to start with the trust document and its impersonal legalese.

Her gaze slid over the standard wording. *The grantor is desirous of creating a trust for the purposes and upon the terms and provisions hereinafter set forth.* Blah, blah, blah. The next section named the successor trustee as Jason R. Andover, and outlined the powers granted to him in carrying out Lillian's wishes. Kelli set her teeth together. She'd assumed the trustee would be Mr. Lewis, her mother's lawyer, or even the bank. That would have been standard. To name a complete stranger as a trustee was highly unusual.

Of course, he's only a stranger to me. What was Jason to you, Lillian?

His handsome face swam before her mind's eye, an angry flush staining his tanned cheeks at her pointed question about his relationship with her mother. Nothing inappropriate, Kelli now felt reasonably sure. He'd said Lillian was like a mother to him, and she found herself bristling again at the thought. Her mother had shared a relationship with someone else that she'd withheld from her own daughter. That stung. But it wasn't Jason's doing. The fault lay with Lillian.

Was Jason named as a beneficiary as well as trustee? Kelli flipped a page and found the section naming the beneficiaries. No, the only two listed were Cougar Bay Zoological Park and Kelli Ann Jackson. *Interesting.*

A few paragraphs later, she found the section outlining the distribution of the assets. Lillian's car and the contents of the house were left unconditionally to Kelli.

She looked up and let her gaze sweep the sterile room. Bare furnishings, no knickknacks, no pictures on the wall. Lillian wasn't into possessions, apparently.

The document went on to outline the conditions Mr. Lewis had described. If Kelli accepted an animal care position at the zoo and remained for six months, and if her performance was deemed acceptable at the sole discretion of the zoo director, she would receive fifty percent of the estate's value.

She shifted on the scratchy sofa and scowled at the document. It specified that the position had to be "an animal care position," which meant she couldn't go to work in the office where she'd be far more comfortable. But even worse was the phrase *at the sole discretion of the zoo director.*

"So, in other words, I could work here for six miserable months, and if Lillian's substitute son doesn't like me, I'll walk away with nothing."

The harshness of her voice rang in the empty house. Her own fierce tone startled her, but not as much as the thought that caused it. Lillian assumed she could be bought, that she'd do the thing she abhorred just for the money. An angry flush warmed her neck.

The next item outlined the provision Mr. Lewis mentioned. If she chose not to accept a position at the zoo, she would receive a cash disbursement of $25,000, and the balance would be forfeited to the zoo.

"So, you didn't leave me penniless. You gave me an out." Kelli's bitter whisper sounded flat in the silent room. Did her mother think that made the rest of this ridiculous document okay? Was that provision supposed to appease Lillian's conscience for the turmoil she knew she would cause her daughter?

The zoo had conditions to meet as well. The adjoining property must be used for expansion of the existing facilities, and must include an African Habitat to house species native to the African continent. The expansion must include a suitable habitat for lions, funded by the estate's liquid assets. Kelli flinched. Lions again. Jason R. Andover must be named as zoo director with an employment contract of one year.

Kelli's lips curved into a grudging smile. She had to admit, Lillian seemed to have thought of everything. Without a time commitment, the zoo could have fired Jason the day after the money was disbursed. A year gave him a chance to prove himself in the position. Then her smile faded. Was that Lillian's idea or Jason's? Just how much input had the handsome new zoo director had into the conditions of this trust?

A soft thud from the other room drew her attention. She stiffened on the sofa. Was someone else in the house? She forced herself to relax. No reason to get jumpy. It was probably the cat. She set the document on the cushion and rose, making her way slowly in bare feet across the carpet.

At the end of a short hallway stood another sterile room, a bathroom without so much as a hand towel to give it a personal touch. Correction. Tucked between the toilet and the vanity, Kelli spied a litter box. She wrinkled her nose. How like Lillian, to give the cat his own bathroom.

The office door stood open to her right, and a glimpse inside bore testimony to Jason's warning. Piles of paper littered the desk and the top of a two-drawer filing cabinet. A wall clock ticked loudly, and Kelli realized she'd been hearing the sound echo in the silent house since she arrived. But nothing stirred in the office. Kelli turned her back on it. There would be time to dig into that soon enough.

She crept toward the room on the opposite side of the bathroom. The place was almost empty. In the far corner stood one of those cat exercise thingies, nearly four feet tall with carpet-covered posts and a couple of platforms. Scattered across the floor were a variety of toys—hot-pink mice and a brightly colored stuffed bird. Apparently, the cat had his own bedroom as well. The orange feline himself—Leo, Jason had called him—was currently amusing himself by batting a rubber ball around the carpet. As Kelli watched, it bounced off the baseboard and created the soft thud she'd heard. Leo leaped after it and pounced, sending it flying in the opposite direction.

Then the cat caught sight of her in the doorway. In a flash, he shot through a crack in the closet's sliding doors and disappeared from sight.

"Fine," Kelli told the cat. "Stay in there, then. Doesn't bother me at all."

Instead of returning to the couch, she crossed the living room. Her suitcase stood where Jason had left it. She stepped past it, into her mother's bedroom.

Thankfully, this room wasn't nearly as messy as the office. Nor was it as antiseptic as the living room. At least there were pictures on the wall, all of them animal shots. Furnishings were sparse and serviceable: a double bed, a dresser, a nightstand. A thin layer of dust covered everything. Kelli knew from the hospital representative who'd called her three days ago that Lillian had been in the hospital for two weeks prior to her death.

And she didn't want them to call me. Didn't even name a next of kin until the end.

Across the room, the door to the bathroom stood open. Kelli started toward it, but a picture on the wall beside her head snagged her gaze. A close-up of a shaggy, golden lion, its mouth opened wide. The camera had captured a perfect shot of the vicious, powerful teeth.

A shudder rippled through Kelli, along with a powerful memory that was still too vivid, even after eighteen years. *What was the matter with that woman? How could she sleep in the same room with a picture like this after what happened?*

Revulsion twisted in her stomach. Wasn't it enough that a lion had destroyed their family? A lion had been the reason Kelli grew up living with Nana instead of in a normal family with a mother and—she closed her eyes—a father. Kelli snatched the picture and set it on the floor, facing the wall. That creature would have to go elsewhere if she was to sleep in here for even one night. She looked around the room. The majority of the pictures seemed to be of lions, a fact that repulsed her and pricked her curiosity at the same time. What could possibly explain Lillian's bizarre fascination with lions? It was sick.

Kelli shook her head. Before bedtime she'd take down all these animal pictures and stash them somewhere. Maybe Leo would like some company in his closet.

Back on the living-room sofa, she picked up the envelope and stared at it. The familiar ache, buried deep in her heart long ago, began to throb. Was this letter Lillian's attempt to explain the actions that had such a devastating effect on her eight-year-old daughter? An attempt to heal the old wounds?

Kelli carefully opened the envelope, aware that her mother had sealed it with her own mouth. A final kiss goodbye.

Dear Kelli,

By now you've learned about the trust. You probably think I'm being mean to you. Maybe I am, but not without a good reason.

Your father and I both gave our lives to the preservation of zoo animals. I promise you, the strength of my dedication is no less than his. Will you give us a mere six months to see if you can get a glimpse of our passion? If I could have convinced you to do it while I was alive, I would have. I just didn't know how. This trust is my way of asking you to share my life.

Only God knows the damage I've done to you. I hope He forgives me. I don't expect you to. Ask somebody to tell you about Cocoa. Maybe you'll understand.

I do love you, Kelli, more than I was ever able to express.

It was signed in her hurried script, *Lillian Mitchell.* Beneath her signature she had written, *Your Mother.* As if Kelli needed the reminder of who she was.

She read the last line again. Tears stung her eyes. Love? Nana loved Kelli and proved it by being there every day as she grew up, by taking care of her, by coming to her band concerts and taking her to Sunday school. Lillian didn't know what love was. She wanted Kelli to share her life?

"It's a little too late for that, isn't it?" Her shout, aimed at the letter, squeaked at the end as her throat squeezed shut. "My childhood is over, and so is your life."

She tossed away the letter. Tears blurred her vision as she watched it flutter to the floor. Once again, Lillian had proved what Kelli had long known: Her precious zoo animals were more important than her own daughter.

"It's all about you, isn't it, Lillian?" She kept her voice low, her whisper masking the sobs that threatened. "Your dedication. Your passion. It's always been about you."

Her gaze fell on the trust document, Lillian's attempt to manipulate her, to *bribe* her. Well, Kelli wouldn't play along with it. She refused to sell her soul for money.

An image of Nana rose in her mind. Frail Nana, who moved slower these days. Who sometimes forgot to turn off the gas oven until the next morning. There would come a time, and it might be soon, when Nana couldn't continue to live alone. Lillian's money would ensure that she didn't have to.

"That's okay." Kelli lifted her chin, her decision made. "We'll manage without it."

She got off the sofa and went to retrieve her cell phone from her purse. Nana would be wondering what was happening, and when Kelli would be returning to Denver.

The zoo was crowded today. Jason passed a string of children in identical yellow T-shirts crowding around the red panda enclosure, and nodded a pleasant greeting at the pair of young women who stood watching them. He'd heard someone from Guest Services say they had a couple of summer camp groups scheduled today. Until a couple of months ago, he would have been assigned the task of introducing them to Samson and the other cats. But that was before Lil got sick enough to hand off some of her duties to him. Now Michael was the zookeeper primarily in charge of big cats.

But Samson had earned a special place in Jason's heart a long time ago. No matter how busy his day, Jason always found time to pay a visit to the lion. That's where he headed now, with Lil's letter folded in his pocket.

Samson dozed on the shaded concrete platform in the corner of his enclosure, as he usually did during the heat of the day.

Jason stood at the external barrier near a mother and her two boys, whose fingers were locked in the chain link. He studied the magnificent beast's golden fur, his shaggy main. As Jason watched, the conspicuous dark tuft at the end of his long tail flicked upward, then collapsed again to its limp position. Besides that, Samson didn't move at all.

"C'mon," one boy said to his brother, his tone heavy with disgust. "Let's go look at the monkeys. At least they jump around."

Jason hid a smile as the trio strolled away. Samson considered himself too regal to perform for a crowd. He was, after all, the king of beasts, even if he was without a pride over which to rule at the moment.

The nearby bench, tucked into a welcome patch of shade, was empty. Jason fought off a stab of guilt and seated himself. A pile of work lay on Lil's desk—*his* desk, unofficially—but that could wait for a few minutes. Here, in front of the animal Lillian had loved so much, was the ideal place to read her letter.

He ripped open the envelope and extracted the single page covered in his late boss's familiar handwriting.

Jason,

I've never been good at telling people how I feel. I'm much better at telling them what to do.

Jason smiled. That was true.

I'm not going to get all gushy, because that will just embarrass you. (I guess I'm beyond being embarrassed now, aren't I?) But I do think you're a fine man, and the best person to become zoo director after me. I trust you to carry on the work I've started. You'll get no higher praise from me than that.

I hope you and Kelli get along. I warn you, she's going to have a hard time with this. I won't ask you to go easy on her, but try

not to make it any harder than it has to be. She carries a lot of
pain. Maybe she'll open up to you one day and tell you about it.
Get Samson out of that cage, Jason. Don't let them take him.

Lillian Mitchell

Jason looked up from the letter, his gaze drawn to Samson's enclosure. Lil's use of the disparaging word *cage* spoke volumes. Samson's home was pathetically small for such a glorious animal. True, it met the Association of Zoos and Aquariums' minimum requirements, barely. But Samson deserved so much more. On that, Lil and Jason had been in complete agreement. Samson was a perfect specimen, healthy and virile, and easily met the AZA's strict breeding qualifications. But without a proper habitat, the AZA would never allow them a female lion, would never approve Cougar Bay's application to initiate a lion breeding program. In fact, because all zoo animals technically belong to AZA, it was within that organization's power to move Samson to another facility, one with a habitat more suitable for breeding. And Lil had been sure they would do it. Her determination not to let that happen had flickered like gray flame in her eyes whenever the subject came up.

Had she taken that determination too far? Kelli's image rose in his mind.

"Maybe she'll open up to you one day and tell you about it." Jason slowly shook his head. "You sound pretty sure she'll accept your conditions, Lil." He wasn't convinced. He'd glimpsed a touch of obstinacy in the set of that lovely chin, much the same as he'd seen her mother display. Kelli Jackson wasn't the kind to be pushed into something she didn't want to do. Surely Lil knew that about her own daughter.

He refolded the letter and slid it back into the envelope. In the days before she died, Lil had made no secret of the fact that she expected him to be ruthless in his execution of her trust.

Even though he'd been reeling from the discovery that she had a daughter, he'd tried to talk her out of the crazy scheme.

"Lil, why don't you just leave the poor kid her half and be done with it?"

The wasted woman in the hospital bed had been a mere shadow of the boss he'd known for years. But she'd leveled a stubborn look on him and rasped with some of her precious remaining breath, "For her own good. Everybody has to face their fears."

"But why me? Surely there's someone else who could do a better job, as trustee and as director."

The soft pat on his hand held so little strength it felt like a breeze. "You'll take care of Samson. Nobody else will."

Jason thrust away the memory and abruptly rose from the bench. He crossed to the chain-link barrier and stared into the lion enclosure. But instead of Samson, he saw a beautiful dark-haired young woman with pain lurking in the gray depths of her eyes. A young woman who would probably end up hating him, according to Lil, although she wouldn't explain why.

Well, seemed he had a knack for rubbing beautiful women the wrong way. Aimee couldn't stand to be in the same room with him.

"This is your fault," he told the lion. "I don't know what fear Kelli has to face, but Lil was right about one thing. She already blames me."

Samson snoozed on, oblivious. Jason put the letter back in his pocket. He was used to taking the blame where women were concerned. If he had to be the bad guy with Lil's daughter, he'd do it. Especially if it meant Samson would get a new home, as Lil and he both wanted.

Chapter Five

*D*espite Kelli's fears, the office wasn't in complete disorder. The top drawer of the filing cabinet held a series of neatly labeled folders containing various zoo records. Those, she would box up and turn over to Jason. But the rest were her responsibility to sort through.

The bottom of the file cabinet and all the desk drawers had served as a catchall into which Lillian had apparently tossed her personal documents: bills, bank statements, even junk mail. Kelli frowned at the piles, her accountant mind trying to perceive her mother's system. After a few minutes, she gave up.

"I must have inherited my organization skills from Daddy," she muttered.

A movement in the doorway drew her attention, and she looked up into Leo's golden gaze. The sound of her voice must have attracted his curiosity. After barely a second of eye contact, the animal dashed away, in the direction of his closet. Kelli chuckled and returned to her task.

"What a mess." *Tsking* in disapproval, she cleared the surface of the desk, then began the tedious process of sorting the clutter into a semblance of order. Time to find out if Lillian's finances were as big a mess as her office.

A couple of hours later, Kelli started to breathe a little easier. Her mother had left surprisingly few outstanding bills. Her medical coverage—the policy was in the bottom drawer of the filing cabinet—was comprehensive. There would probably be a few medical bills, but the bulk of the treatment would be covered. And she'd carried mortgage insurance on the house.

"A free and clear title. How nice for the zoo." She didn't bother to filter the sarcasm out of her voice. The cat didn't care, and there was no one else to hear.

Her mother had carried several credit cards, and Kelli felt a grudging respect as she inspected the statements. Lillian paid the balances off every month.

The ringing of her cell phone in the other room pierced through the empty house. Kelli jumped, startled, then hurried to answer it. A glance at the screen showed an unfamiliar number, and she almost let the call go to voice mail. But it was a local area code. Might be the attorney.

"Hello?"

"Kelli, this is Jason Andover." The low voice drawled in her ear. "We just got a call from the hospital where your mother ... uh, died." He sounded apologetic, like he hated to mention the fact. "They still have Lil's stuff. Her wallet and so on."

Kelli glanced toward the office. She'd seen the credit card statements, but now that she thought of it, no cards. Lillian must have taken the things to the hospital with her. Kelli had already made a list of companies to call with the numbers of the accounts to be closed out, but the credit cards should be cut up, the blank checks destroyed.

She leaned against the countertop. "Of course. I'll go pick them up. Can you give me directions to the hospital?"

"Well ..." He turned the word into two syllables. "Driving there can be a little tricky. How about if I run you over?"

Kelli straightened to attention. Why would he want to do that? Was he simply making a nice gesture, or did he have another reason?

A thought occurred to her, and she allowed herself a grim smile. He probably wanted to find out if she'd made a decision about staying on for the required six months. He wanted to know whether his precious zoo would inherit the full $1.4 million, or only half that amount.

She allowed a chill to creep into her tone. "I can handle it, if you'll just tell me where it is."

A pause. "All right, if that's what you want. Got a pencil?"

She retrieved her purse and wrote his directions on the back of an ATM receipt. It actually did sound like a complicated drive, especially in an unfamiliar city and in a car she'd never driven. Maybe she'd been a little hasty in turning down his offer.

"When you get off at the exit, turn right and stay on that road for about, oh, five or six miles. You'll see St. Mark's on your left." A moment of silence. "I really don't mind driving you over."

Kelli hesitated. "I'd hate to take you away from your work."

His low laugh sent a delightful and completely unwelcome ripple through her. "Trust me, I'll be here for a long time tonight. An hour or so away won't hurt a thing."

"Well, if you're sure." She sank against the counter, relieved. "When do you want to go?"

"It's almost four. If we leave now, we'll miss the worst of the rush-hour traffic."

"Do you want me to come to the office?"

"It'll be faster if I drive around and pick you up. Give me five minutes."

Kelli's hand lingered on the phone after she hung up. No doubt he had an ulterior motive for his good deed, but even so, it was a nice offer.

As she turned away, she spied two bowls tucked in a corner of the kitchen, one empty, one with a quarter inch of water in the bottom. Ah, no wonder Leo had ventured out of his closet earlier. He was probably hungry. What did the creature eat?

Knowing Lillian's affection for all things feline, he probably got fresh salmon or something.

A quick inspection of the cabinets revealed a package of macaroni, three cans of green beans, and half-full bag of dry cat food. Kelli dumped food in the empty bowl and put fresh water in the other one. That gave her just enough time to run a brush through her hair and smooth on some lipstick before Jason arrived to pick her up.

Not that she needed to dress up for her mother's substitute son. Just that she wanted to look her best in front of the hospital staff.

Jason wracked his brain to come up with a conversation starter during the drive to the hospital. Small talk wasn't his forte. Especially small talk with attractive women who obviously distrusted him. Kelli situated herself on the far edge of the passenger seat, as far away from him as she could get, and stared with a stony expression through the windshield.

The ability to maintain long periods of silence was another trait she shared with her mother.

"So, you live in Denver?"

Her gaze slid sideways for a moment. She nodded once, then looked forward again.

"What do you do out there?"

After a pause that went on long enough to make him think she wasn't going to answer, she did. "I'm an accountant in a private firm."

"That sounds like interesting work." Actually, it didn't. He couldn't imagine anything duller than being stuck behind a desk, staring at numbers all day. "Did you go to school out there?"

"Yes, I went to the University of Denver."

He executed a turn off the freeway. "I used to work with a guy who studied Animal Technology there. He's probably close to your age. Maybe you knew him."

"I doubt it." Her lips tightened into a hard line. "I make it a point to stay away from people who work with animals."

Jason fought to keep his expression bland. Had he just been purposefully insulted? Seemed so. This girl was holding a serious grudge against someone. Lillian, probably. What could have happened between them to cause such a rift? And why was she determined to take it out on him?

Kelli turned her head toward him, her eyes softer than a moment before. "I'm sorry. That was rude. I just—" She looked down at the hands she clasped in her lap. "I've had almost no contact with animals since I was a little girl. I prefer to keep it that way."

"Why?" The question shot out before he could stop it. "What happened to make you hate animals?"

Her head tilted sideways, curiosity etched on her face. "Didn't my mother tell you anything about me?"

"Not a word. In fact—" He faced forward, not able to look her in the face as he admitted, "I didn't even know you existed until two days before Lil died. None of us at the zoo did."

"Two days *before?* Why didn't you call me, so I could have seen her before the end?" Her question held a note of accusation.

His final argument with Lil was still fresh in his mind. He'd wanted to do just that, but she'd remained adamant. "She made me promise not to. I didn't even know your name or where you lived." He paused and then went on in a quieter voice. "I could have contacted Daniel Lewis and had him get in touch with you. But I thought I could convince her. I thought she had more time."

The silence returned as he covered the last few miles to the hospital. When Jason had parked the car in the main parking lot and turned off the engine, Kelli spoke again.

"It's not your fault." A sad smile twitched at the edges of her mouth. "She didn't want to see me. No surprise there."

Her shoulders drooped, and a wave of compassion took Jason by surprise. Memories of Dad rushed back to him. How awful to have missed those last few days with him. And yet, those had been the most difficult days of his long illness. At least Lil's decline had been blessedly shorter, although certainly no less painful.

He cleared his throat. "Maybe she didn't want you to see her. She didn't exactly look herself right there at the end." He didn't elaborate. No sense describing the shocking change that occurred in the last two weeks of Lil's life as she succumbed to the disease. Jason wished he could erase the sight from his memory.

"Maybe." She turned sideways in the seat to watch him through narrowed eyes. "You didn't know the conditions of her trust?"

"I knew some of them." He held his gaze steady under her scrutiny, his hands still clutching the steering wheel. "I knew she was planning to offer the zoo an incentive to accept me as her replacement, and about the land and the expansion project. And I knew she'd made some provisions for someone else. I just didn't know who, until two days before the end."

"My existence must have been an unpleasant shock, then."

His spine stiffened with a jerk. What was she accusing him of? "I didn't assume she'd left me anything personally, if that's what you're implying."

She studied him for a long moment, then gave a brief nod. "Sorry. There's just so much I don't understand." A brittle laugh escaped her lips as she leaned forward to pick up the purse at her feet. "Not that it matters. In a few days I'll be back in Denver, where I'll fade into anonymity again."

"So you're not going to stay? Not even for six months?"

Her smile became brittle. "Not even for six *days*. My mother underestimated me." Her chin rose. "I will not be bought."

She opened the door and exited the car. Jason stayed in his seat for a long moment to let her decision sink in. The zoo would receive Lil's entire estate. Once Kelli's half of the assets were liquidated, Cougar Bay would have enough money in the fund to begin construction on the African Lion Habitat. Samson would have a new home. It was really going to happen.

Then why was he so disappointed?

The moment the elevator doors glided open, a strong antiseptic smell stung Kelli's nostrils. She stepped onto a sparkling white floor and paused to read the sign on the wall in front of her. Jason didn't hesitate, but took off down the wide corridor to the right, obviously familiar with the place.

He probably visited Lillian several times in her weeks here.

A bitter taste invaded Kelli's mouth at the thought. He'd visited, while Kelli herself had been left out at her mother's request.

He stopped and turned when he noticed she wasn't beside him. "It's just down here."

She nodded and hurried after him, her eyes fixed politely ahead to avoid looking into the rooms she passed. The sound of voices drifted toward her through the open doorways. Halfway down the corridor, they approached a nurse's station on the right, where a woman in pink scrubs sat in a rolling chair, tapping on a computer keyboard. She looked up. Recognition flashed onto her face when she caught sight of Jason, and she greeted him with a nod. Her gaze slid to Kelli and a smile lit her features. She stood and extended her hand.

"Hello. I'm Terri Wainright. And you're Ms. Mitchell's daughter."

The hand felt warm. "That's right. Kelli Jackson."

"It's nice to meet you. I was your mother's nurse on the day shift." The woman's expression sobered. "I'm so sorry for your loss."

"Thank you." Kelli felt like an impostor accepting the sympathy of this woman who'd cared for Lillian during her final days. Surely, that was a daughter's responsibility. She looked down at the floor.

"I have her things right in here." Terri crossed to a doorway behind the nurse's station. In a moment she returned carrying a white plastic bag with handles. "She didn't have much with her when she arrived."

Kelli took the bag. She could feel the contents through the sturdy plastic. Clothes and a hard, flat object in the bottom. She set the bag on the counter and opened the handles to peer inside. A green cotton T-shirt and a pair of jeans lay on top. She pushed them aside and pulled out an inexpensive leather wallet.

"She didn't have a purse?"

Nurse Terri shrugged. "That's all she brought with her."

Beside Kelli, Jason leaned an arm on the high counter. "I never saw Lil carry a purse, only that wallet."

Kelli opened it and inspected the contents. Three credit cards, as she'd expected. A few dollars in cash. An insurance card. And...

She swallowed against a suddenly dry throat. A driver's license. She slid the card out and studied the small image of her mother. Same straight gray hair. Same eyes. Same lean face. No, not exactly the same. There were more lines in evidence, and her cheeks had thinned to the point of gauntness. She'd lost weight since Kelli saw her last. How many years ago was that? Four. Lillian had flown to Denver for Kelli's college graduation.

Oh, Lillian. Unexpected tears stung Kelli's eyes. *If only I'd known, I wouldn't have let so much time pass.*

The nurse and Jason were both watching her. Blinking to clear her eyes, Kelli shoved the license back into the wallet and snapped it shut. When she put it back in the bag, her fingers touched a sharp edge buried beneath the clothing.

"What's this?"

She grasped the object and pulled it out. It was a picture frame, the inexpensive drugstore kind with a cardboard stand on the back to prop it upright. When Kelli turned it over, her heart twisted in her chest. The face that laughed up at her was achingly familiar. A larger version of this same photograph hung in a place of honor on Nana's living room wall. Daddy.

"There should be another one." Terri pulled the bag toward her and reached inside to extract a second frame, identical to the first. "There it is."

Kelli took the picture with numb fingers. She stared, unable to tear her gaze away from the image of herself dressed in a cap and gown, laughing into the camera with her father's smile. Tucked in the corner was a smaller photo, Kelli's second-grade school picture. Same smile, only with a hint of sadness in the eyes and a gap where the front teeth had been. Her last school picture before she went to live with Nana.

Terri's voice was soft. "She kept those with her constantly at the end."

Jason peered sideways at them. "She wouldn't show them to me until two days before she died. When she told me about—" He gulped and shot a quick glance at the nurse. "You know."

"She was hugging them when she passed." Terri placed a warm hand on Kelli's arm. "I don't know what happened between you, but I know she loved you very much."

The happy images blurred as tears filled her eyes. Was it true? Did the mother she always thought indifferent really love her? Or was it only the looming specter of a solitary death that caused Lillian to regret abandoning her only child?

A tear slid down her cheek, followed quickly by another. Kelli couldn't bear to put down the pictures long enough to wipe them away, so she let them go.

Oh, Mom! Why didn't we fix this before it was too late?

Or was it too late? Would this crazy condition of Lillian's trust help her to finally understand what had gone wrong between them? If she agreed, maybe she would discover, once and for all, if the fault had lain with Lillian or with her.

A tear dropped from her chin onto Daddy's picture, followed a second later by another. Jason put an arm awkwardly around her shoulders and squeezed. She found his silent embrace oddly comforting and leaned into his warmth.

In the next moment, she stiffened. No! She couldn't let her guard down around Jason Andover, even for an instant. No matter how nice he seemed, she must remember where this man's loyalties lay. He was a zookeeper and he would always choose his precious animals over everyone else. Just like her parents.

Well, she'd show him. Even if it killed her, she'd last the whole six months. And then she'd walk away without a backward glance.

She stepped sideways, out of his reach. Still clutching the photographs, she lifted her face to look up at Jason. "I've changed my mind. I'm staying."

Chapter Six

*J*ason arrived at the zoo at seven o'clock Friday morning, like he always did, and took his customary walk around the grounds to check on the animals. Everything looked normal, nobody injured or sickly. He examined the repair job on the wolves' fence, satisfied that it seemed to be holding Bob, their resident escape artist, in place. The goats bleated and kicked up a dust storm as they trotted around excitedly. Samson paced the length of his enclosure, eyes fixed on Jason as he passed, as did the cougars. The capuchin monkeys rushed toward his side of their exhibit, calling to him as he strode by.

"Hang on, fellas, food is on the way," he promised.

The radio on Jason's belt erupted with sound. Angela, from the office.

"Jason, Raul just called. He sprained his ankle last night. Won't be in today."

He stopped on the path, digesting the news. Raul, the fiercely possessive zookeeper who'd been at Cougar Bay longer than anyone else, ruled the Small Animal building like a tyrant. He even came in on his days off to check on "his animals." The man's injury must be severe to keep him away from his beloved charges.

Jason conducted a quick mental review of the day's staffing chart as he unclipped his radio. Each keeper took care of a group of animals from a specific natural habitat. They developed a relationship with each animal in their care, feeding them and cleaning up after them regularly, so they could spot a potential problem before anyone else from changes in the animal's behavior or eating habits. Of course, Cougar Bay made sure the keepers were cross-trained, so a person could step in to care for other animals during the regular keeper's absence, a policy Lil had implemented long before Jason joined the team.

The lemurs in the exhibit up ahead saw him stop walking and, alert to the change in the daily routine, raised their voices to a screech as Jason pressed the radio button to answer to Angela.

"When Stephanie gets in, let her know she needs to pick up Small Animals today."

Radio static and then Angela's voice. "She's covering the Canyon and Penguins for Erica today."

Great. And the other keepers were already stretched thin to cover a couple of vacations and the absence created by Jason's reassignment to the director position. They were going to be short-handed on a Friday, the busiest day of the week outside of weekends.

Besides that, Jason had planned to team up Kelli on her first day with Stephanie, the most outgoing and friendliest of the keepers on staff, but he couldn't saddle an already-overworked keeper with a newbie. Especially one with no training and a chip on her shoulder when it came to animals.

Well, he'd just have to take care of the Small Animal building himself. And Kelli would have to hang with him. A memory surfaced, of her pulling away from him at the hospital last night. He didn't know what he'd been thinking to put his arm around her like that. She'd just looked so sad, so forlorn, with tears running unchecked down her cheeks. Until he offered a simple gesture of comfort. Then she'd stiffened like a Popsicle.

She wouldn't like working with him today.

"Tough," he told Casper the cockatoo as he passed. "She'll have to get used to it."

Casper fixed Jason with a shiny black eye as he spoke into the radio. "If Kelli Jackson arrives before I get back to the office, tell her I'll be there shortly. Give her a new hire packet and let her start filling out forms while she waits."

A short pause met that news. Then, "You mean Lil's daughter? She's coming to work here?"

Jason allowed a smile to creep onto his face. The news would make the rounds faster than a cheetah chasing a rabbit. "That's right. She starts work as an assistant keeper today."

Angela was silent as she digested the revelation. Then, "There's a story behind that and I want to hear it."

Jason shook his head. Of course Angela would itch to hear all about it. And as soon as she knew, everyone else would, too. Nice girl, but chatty. Well, Jason didn't intend to say a word about the conditions outlined in Lil's trust. Let Kelli handle that however she wanted.

"Just have her fill out the paperwork and tell her I'll be there shortly."

"Will do."

As he clipped the radio back onto his belt, Jason stopped beside a macaw cage. Bongo, a beautiful blue and gold, continued grooming beneath a wing and ignored him.

"She'll just be another employee," he told the bird. "If she thinks she's going to get special treatment because she's Lil's daughter, she's wrong. She's going to clean enclosures like everyone else."

Only, she wasn't like everyone else. For a second last night when he'd pulled Kelli close to his side, he'd felt something. Like a warm breeze had blown through the cold, empty space inside him. For one moment, he wondered how it would feel to really hold Kelli in his arms.

He swiveled from the cage and strode away quickly, as though he could leave the thought behind with Bongo. He had a lousy track record with women, proven by the fact that Aimee couldn't stand to be near him. Better to stick with something easier to handle, like porcupines.

Kelli signed her name at the bottom of the I-9 form and clicked the pen shut. There. She was now an official employee of Cougar Bay Zoological Park.

Are you happy, Lillian?

Her mind echoed with her boss's angry words on the phone last night when she called to request a six-month leave of absence. The only way she'd managed to calm him down was to agree to continue to work part-time for him at night. Actually, she'd been relieved at the arrangement. Stepping away from her life as an accountant was a huge move, a little too final for her comfort. This way she could keep her long-time clients without worrying that whoever Gary hired to take her place would mess things up for the more complicated accounts. And besides, the work would give her something satisfying to do in the evenings. Working in a zoo certainly wouldn't tax her mental energies.

Jason came into the zoo office as she handed the completed paperwork across the desk to Angela.

"All done?" He nodded toward the packet of papers.

Angela fanned the forms, eyeing each one quickly. "Everything looks good." She smiled up at Kelli. "Welcome to Cougar Bay. I'll get your name tag ordered and it'll be here in a few days. Here's a couple of the shirts everyone in Animal Care wears. Will a medium work for you?"

Angela picked up two folded tan shirts, identical to the one Jason wore, and extended them across the desk.

Kelli managed not to scowl as she took them. "Thank you." She shifted her gaze to Jason. "So, what's on the agenda for today?"

He opened the door and gestured for her to precede him. The heat slapped at her when she left the air-conditioned office. And the humidity! Her lungs felt heavy, weighed down with the sticky moisture in the air she inhaled. The atmosphere in Denver never felt like this. And it was only eight-thirty in the morning.

Jason walked in the same direction they'd taken yesterday, and Kelli fell in beside him.

"Normally, I'd sit you down in a room with a television and DVD player and let you watch the training videos. Unfortunately, we're short-staffed today, so I need your help in the Small Animal building."

She gave him a wary sideways look. "What kind of animals are those?"

"Oh, there's a bunch of them. Rabbits, meerkats, squirrel monkeys. Some of the smaller exotic birds. You'll see."

She breathed a little easier. That didn't sound so bad. She could handle feeding a few rabbits.

He worked his long-legged stride to full advantage on the concrete path. Kelli had to hurry to keep up with him. "I've never taken a job before without knowing the salary and benefits. How much am I being paid?"

"Eight-fifty an hour."

"What?" She scowled. "I could make more at a fast-food restaurant."

His eyebrows arched. "You're lucky you're getting a paycheck at all. Most interns aren't paid."

"I'm an intern?" She didn't like the sound of that. She was a CPA, for goodness' sake, not some trainee dog walker. "I have a college degree, you know."

The fact failed to impress him. "Some of our keepers have several. Even interns have typically just earned their degree, or will within a few months. They're here to get experience working with exotic animals and they're happy to do it for free." They approached a low, one-story building with Small Animals lettered over the door. Jason leaned forward, then paused with his fingers on the handle. "Your official title is Assistant Keeper, just so no one gets upset. We never hire an inexperienced person as a keeper. You might want to keep that in mind when you meet the others."

Terrific. She was going to be known as a special case, and judging from the caution she read in Jason's face, not everyone would be happy to welcome her into the fold just because she was Lillian's daughter. Well, forewarned was forearmed.

She acknowledged the warning with a nod. "Good to know."

He swung open the door and gestured for her to enter. She did, then skidded to a stop just over the threshold as though she'd encountered a physical barrier.

"Eeew." Her nose wrinkled. "What is that smell?"

Not one smell, actually, but a combination of several revolting odors, blended into an eye-stinging stench. Wet fur, ammonia, and the same foul stink that had come from Leo's litter box this morning magnified by a factor of a hundred. She resisted the urge to pinch her nostrils shut like a peevish child.

"Awful, isn't it?" A sympathetic grin stole across Jason's well-shaped mouth. "Trust me, you'll get used to it in no time."

She found herself returning his contagious grin. If she was going to be stuck here for six months, she'd need allies. And he would make a really nice-looking ally.

But then she remembered who he was. And what he was. And what he would gain for his beloved zoo if she failed. Trust him? She wiped the smile from her face. Not in a million years.

"I'll never get used to this," she told him.

From the look in his eyes, he knew she didn't mean the smell. He held her gaze for a long moment, then gave a nearly imperceptible nod.

"All right, then. Come with me and let's get started."

She followed him down a wide hallway, past several glass-fronted enclosures. A pair of rabbits hopped around a floor covered with straw. Next door, a group of meerkats raced across a sandy floor or climbed on a structure made to resemble large rocks. One stood at attention on curved hind legs, its long neck extended and front paws dangling like hands in front, scanning its domain with eyes surrounded by black fur like a bandit's mask. It looked just like the television show she'd surfed over on the Discovery Channel. Beyond that, a half dozen little monkeys performed wild acrobatics on the leafless branches of a wooden tree that stretched from one end of the enclosure to the other.

The building extended on, with windowed exhibits on both sides and an exit at the far end. Jason went to a door in the center, which he unlocked with the ring of keys he extracted from his bulging pocket.

"In here is where we do diets."

She followed him into a cramped workroom. A high, stainless-steel counter lined one wall, a deep sink at the far end. In the center stood a rack of plastic bins, each one labeled in careful black lettering. More plastic bins lined one wall, and to her left stood a side-by-side refrigerator/freezer. The back wall consisted of a row of metal cages, all empty. The bare concrete floor sloped toward a drain near the sink.

Kelli scanned the labels on the plastic bins. Some of the names were mysteries, but she spotted a curious one.

"Dog food? You have dogs in here?"

Jason opened the refrigerator and answered as he rummaged inside. "No dogs, but some of the carnivores eat it soaked in water." He emerged with a plastic lunchroom tray piled with fruits and vegetables. "Grab that knife over there, would you?"

Kelli found a butcher knife where he indicated, but when she tried to hand it to him, he shook his head. "You'll need it to chop the vegetables. These charts tell you exactly how much each animal gets."

He pointed to a series of laminated pages tacked to the wall above the counter listing dozens of animal species and the food to be served to each. He set a battery-operated kitchen scale in front of her, put a white plastic bowl on it and tapped the first chart.

"Start at the top and work your way down."

First on the list were the meerkats. Kelli studied the ingredients. Preparing each animal's diet was sort of like following a recipe. Forty grams of mixed fruit, forty grams of yams, forty grams of carrots. Then—

"King mealworms?"

He snapped his fingers. "Oh, yeah. They're up here." He lifted a white plastic tub down from the top of the refrigerator and set it on the counter beside the vegetable tray. Kelli peeked inside and her stomach quivered. Hundreds of fat, hard-shelled worms, some nearly as long as her finger, writhed in a disgusting mass.

She turned toward Jason and scrunched her features. "That. Is. Revolting."

The slow grin curled his lips again. "You get used to it."

He disappeared through another doorway, and Kelli got busy chopping yams, carrots, apples and oranges. When she had everything measured out in the bowl, it looked great. Appetizing, even. Like something she might fix for herself at a salad bar. Until—

She looked around for a scoop, or a spoon, or something to use to get the mealworms. Nothing. *Terrific.* She picked up the plastic tub and angled a corner over the bowl, then used the edge of her knife to scoop out worms.

The numbers on the scale jumped faster than she expected, and before she knew it, she'd added sixty-five grams of king mealworms instead of the required fifty. They writhed disgustingly on top of her fruit-and-veggie salad. In vain, she searched for a spoon or some other utensil to remove a few.

With a gulp, she scrunched her nose to brace herself and used a thumb and forefinger to grab a couple of nasty, wriggling worms. Her stomach lurched as they squirmed between her fingers before she tossed them back into the tub.

Jason's laughter startled her. "You should see the look on your face. Didn't you ever play with bugs when you were a kid?"

She turned to find him watching from the doorway. A flush warmed her neck at the sight of his teasing smile. "Certainly not."

"Well, I did. In fact, one of my mother's favorite stories is the time I was out digging in a field near our house and came home with my pockets bulging. She thought I'd filled my pants with dirt, but when she asked me what I had, I pulled out a wriggling handful and announced proudly, 'Worms!'" He chuckled. "Night crawlers are a lot slimier than mealworms."

Kelli couldn't stop a smile. He must have been such a cute little boy, with that golden brown hair and that contagious grin. She hid her smile by turning back toward her scale and cautiously removing a final worm. "There. Perfect. Now, the last thing is a half teaspoon of vitamins."

Jason pulled a plastic container off a shelf and sprinkled a dusting of white powder on top of the food. "You get to where you can eyeball the amount."

When he returned the vitamins to the shelf, his bare arm brushed Kelli's. His skin felt warm, and hers tingled where they touched. Last night, that very arm had been around her, firm and comforting and—

She cleared her throat as she edged away. "So, next on the list are rock cavies, whatever those are."

"You'll love the rock cavies. They're round and furry and cute, like pudgy guinea pigs."

Kelli scanned the food chart. "At least they don't eat worms. And before you say it, I know. I'll get used to it."

He gave a deep laugh that filled the room.

A small smile crept onto Kelli's face as she reached for a carrot to chop for the cavies.

By the time she reached the last animal on the list, the bat-eared fox, touching the king mealworms no longer made her stomach lurch. Yams seemed to be a staple, as did carrots, apples and bananas. The skunk—descented, Jason assured her—got half a hardboiled egg. Bowls of food lined the counter, some of it tempting enough to set off a hungry rumble in her stomach.

He eyed her handiwork. "Good work."

Kelli caught herself just before she preened at the praise. Chopping a few vegetables wasn't rocket science. It would have been hard to mess that up. Still, she couldn't help a flush of satisfaction at Jason's approval.

Then she noticed the caution etched on his face. "The next part isn't as pleasant."

Kelli was instantly on guard. "What's that?"

He picked up a dustpan, a paint scraper and a scrub brush. "We get to clean the animals' enclosures."

Kelli twisted her lips and scowled. *Lovely. I'm being paid eight-fifty an hour to pick up poop.*

Jason lifted a shoulder. "It's part of the job."

With a heavy sigh, she held out a hand for the dustpan. "I suppose it is. All right, then. Let's do it."

They loaded as many of the bowls as they could fit on the top shelf of a rolling utility cart and left the small room.

"We'll start with the porcupines," Jason told her as he guided the cart to the far end of the building.

"Because they're at the end?"

"Because they're so cute."

"Porcupines are cute?" She gave him a disbelieving stare.

His smile held a touch of pride. "Ours are."

When they reached the last exhibit, Kelli examined the pair of occupants with a growing sense of dismay.

"I thought this was the *Small* Animal building."

These creatures definitely didn't qualify. Their black bodies were at least three feet long, with an impressive cluster of white quills that protruded behind them like peacock feathers and made them appear even bigger. When they caught sight of Kelli and Jason, both of them waddled over to a panel on the far side of their enclosure.

"They're about average-sized for African crested porcupines." Jason turned a grin on her. "You ready to meet your first animals?"

Kelli eyed the spiny creatures now standing on their hind legs, their front paws against the glass while they watched her through beady black eyes. "Are they safe? They won't shoot their spines at me?"

"That's a myth. Porkies don't shoot their spines. Mostly they rattle them to frighten their enemies." He selected several large chunks of carrots out of the biggest bowls on the cart. "But we're not their enemies. Nothing to worry about."

Kelli followed him to a door beside the enclosure and waited as he unlocked it. It opened onto a room about the size of a closet. Half the space had been partitioned off, and she could see the outline of a panel separating it from the porcupines' exhibit. A second panel opened into the enclosure from the front of the closet.

Jason moved as far inside as possible and gestured for her to join him. "We never open up an animal's enclosure with the keeper's closet door open. It's a safety procedure."

With a gulp, Kelli stepped inside. He reached beyond her and pulled the door closed. The only light came from the cracks around the two panels leading into the exhibit. She shrank against the rear wall, trying to take up as little of the limited space as possible, but even so, she couldn't avoid brushing against Jason as she moved.

His voice sounded soft and alarmingly close. "Now, I'm going to open this panel and we'll go inside. They'll be curious about you, but don't be afraid. They won't hurt you."

"Are you sure?" Fear quivered in her voice and she was glad for the darkness so Jason couldn't see the panic that must surely be evident on her face. She had managed to avoid contact with animals for eighteen years, but that was about to come to an end in a close encounter with a couple of ginormous pincushions.

A strong, comforting hand gripped her upper arm. "I'm positive. Trust me."

There he went again, asking her to trust him. She didn't, not even a little bit. But at the moment, she had no choice.

She heard a metallic rattle as he unlatched the front panel. Then he backed up to swing the board inward and pressed against her for an instant. Kelli's head buzzed as blood rushed through her veins, maybe from Jason's touch, or maybe from the knowledge that there were large, prickly animals on the other side of that wall. She didn't know which and didn't have time to spend in contemplation. In the next instant, the panel swung wide and light flooded the keeper closet. Jason, moving slowly, stepped over a two-feet-high lip and into the enclosure. The pair of spiny creatures huddled around his legs, sniffing his shoes. He turned and extended a hand toward her.

"Come on. Don't be afraid."

Her mouth tasted cottony and she couldn't even manage to swallow. Gulping a fortifying breath, she reached out and grabbed Jason's hand. He might be the enemy, and she didn't trust him, but at least he was human. At the moment he was the only semi-familiar thing she had to hold on to.

And hold she did. Even after she eased into the porcupine's enclosure, she continued to clutch his hand with a death grip as the curious animals nosed around her shoes.

"This is Gasira." Jason pointed to one of the creatures. "Her name means *bold* and *courageous*."

The second porcupine finished its inspection of her shoes and, to Kelli's horror, rose up on its hind legs and rested a pudgy paw on her thigh so it could nose around her waist. Terrified to move, Kelli froze and stared down at the creature's face. Pink skin surrounded its small, dark eyes, the rest covered in coarse black hair. The delicate curve of pink ears was visible, flat against the narrow head. The long hair became white at the end, and swept back from the animal's forehead in a sort of bouffant to blend with the black-and-white spines covering the lower two-thirds of its body.

A similarity struck her so strongly that a nervous laugh escaped her lips. "That hair makes it look like an old-fashioned televangelist."

Jason chuckled. "He does, doesn't he? His name is Baya. That means *ugly* in Swahili." He released her hand to unzip a pouch at his waist.

Kelli examined Baya. His paw rested against her jeans with a light touch, while his slitted nostrils twitched upward. "I'm afraid the name fits."

"Nah. Baya's a fine-looking fellow, isn't he, Gasira?" He spoke to the female now nosing his knee as he extracted two chunks of carrots. "Here, give him one of these."

Kelli extended the carrot to Baya with a tentative gesture, amazed when he took it gently from her fingers. He dropped to all fours and turned his back on her, his spines spread. Alarmed, she backed away.

"What's he doing?"

Jason shrugged, unconcerned. "Just guarding his food, mostly from Gasira. She's a pig. She'll gulp down her own and try to steal his if he's not careful."

Kelli's fear began to slip away as she watched the two eat, fascinated in spite of herself. She'd never admit it to Jason, but it was kind of cute the way they held the carrots between their leathery front paws and gnawed with long, rabbit-like teeth. Sure enough, Gasira finished hers first and began to edge toward Baya, but he shifted his body so she encountered only his spines.

When they'd finished, Jason reached into the closet and pulled a rope, which raised the second panel and opened an entrance into the partitioned-off section.

"This is called a shift," he explained. "We have one for almost every animal at the zoo, except for some of the smaller ones who shift into crates. Part of their training is to learn to shift so we can have access to their enclosures without them being inside."

Sure enough, the moment the board rose, both Baya and Gasira waddled obediently inside. Jason rewarded each with another carrot before lowering the panel.

"Now we can clean without them underfoot." His lips twisted into an apologetic grimace. "This is the fun part."

He stepped outside to retrieve the dustpan, scraper and an empty bucket, which he brought inside to her. Then he pointed beyond an obstacle course of fake boulders and tree stumps, where a nest of straw filled the far corner of the enclosure.

"That's their preferred area," he explained.

Preferred for what? Kelli started to ask, but then she realized what he meant. Part of the straw was disgustingly wet and dirty. Setting an iron guard on her stomach, Kelli took the items from Jason's hands and started resolutely for the corner. He pulled a pair of rubber gloves out of his back pocket and offered them.

55

As she pulled on the gloves, he asked casually, "How're you doing with the smell?"

With a start, Kelli realized she hadn't noticed the odor for some time. Here she was, up to her ankles in porcupine poop, and the smell wasn't gagging her. *The inside of my nostrils have probably been permanently damaged from ammonia burns or something like that. I'll never be able to smell properly again.* A second thought followed. *He was right, doggone it. You do get used to the smell.*

But to Jason she only replied coolly, "It still stinks in here."

He laughed and left her alone to do her dirty job.

Chapter Seven

By the time they finished with the last exhibit, Jason decided Kelli didn't look quite as haughty as before. The zoo had opened to the public at nine, and there was something humbling about scrubbing the filthy floor of an animal enclosure on your hands and knees while a dozen preadolescent children stood with their noses pressed to the glass, making loud comments about the "great big monkey" inside. At least all the animals had cooperated and shifted without incident. Sometimes the squirrel monkeys liked to be difficult, but even they'd gone into their shift without too much trouble.

The high-pitched voices of shrieking children echoed off the concrete floor and glass windows of the Small Animal building as he led Kelli back into the workroom. He stepped inside and closed the door behind them, cutting off the worst of the noise. She sighed in obvious relief.

"Loud, aren't they?" Jason pushed the cart into a corner and emptied the bucket full of fouled straw into a garbage can. "That's why I prefer early mornings and late nights, when I have the place to myself."

"Still, I suppose they pay the bills." She peeled off her rubber gloves and tossed them in the can.

"That's true."

She sank against the counter and folded her arms across her chest. "So, they're all fed and cleaned. What's next?"

Jason resisted the urge to remove a piece of straw from the unruly dark curls that hung around her shoulders. "Lunch."

"I'm not hungry yet." She glanced at her watch. "It's only eleven thirty."

"Not us. Them." He jerked his head toward the door to indicate the inhabitants of the Small Animal building.

Dismay colored her features. "They eat lunch, too?"

He laughed. "Some of them. Look here." He lifted one of the charts on the wall and showed her the page beneath it listing PM Diets and Snacks. "In the wild many of these animals hunt for food all day. We try to keep their lives in captivity as close to their natural environment as possible."

With a loud sigh, she reached for the butcher knife she'd used earlier. "Okay. Bring on the yams."

The sound of a key in the lock made Jason turn as the door opened. A bushy gray beard entered first, followed by a familiar face and rotund body.

"Ah, Pete." Jason nodded a greeting at the man. "Glad you stopped by. I have someone I'd like you to meet. This is Kelli Jackson, a new assistant keeper who just started today. Kelli, Dr. Pete Morgan, our veterinarian."

Kelli shifted the knife to her left hand so she could shake Pete's with her right. "Nice to meet you, Dr. Morgan."

He dismissed the formality with a wave. "Call me Pete." His blue eyes appeared twice their normal size as he peered at her from behind thick lenses. "You look familiar. We've met before, haven't we?"

Kelli shot a quick glance at Jason before answering. "I don't think so, but you might have seen me yesterday at the memorial service."

Recognition dawned on Pete's face and his expression became sorrowful. "You're Lil's daughter. My dear, I'm so sorry for your loss."

The corners of her mouth twitched upward briefly as she mumbled, "Thank you," and then she looked awkwardly at the floor. Jason knew how she felt. When Dad died earlier this year, everyone wanted to tell him how sorry they were. People meant well, of course, but no one else could possibly know what you were going through. Of course, he'd been close to Dad. Kelli barely knew her mother, which must make it even more difficult to accept the sympathy of strangers.

"So, Pete, are you making your rounds?"

"Yes, yes." The man fumbled with the papers on a clipboard, tilting his head upward to examine them through the bottom half of his bifocals. "I wanted to check on the desert cottontail. Is Raul here?" His gaze circled the room, as though expecting Raul to step out of a corner.

"He sprained his ankle last night," Jason told him.

Pete winced. "Oh, that's too bad. He called yesterday to report that one of the cottontails was lethargic and may be sickening. Did you notice any odd behavior this morning?"

Jason shook his head. "They both appeared to be fine."

The radio at Jason's belt erupted into life. Cameron's voice. "Jason, you'd better get over here."

Cameron was the keeper in charge of primates. Was something wrong with one of the animals? He unclipped the radio and answered. "What's wrong?"

"There's an AZA inspector here."

Jason's pulse kicked up a notch. Cougar Bay was in the process of completing the application for reaccreditation with the Association for Zoos and Aquariums, but it wasn't due until September first. The formal inspection, a nerve-racking experience that kept every staff member biting their nails for months, wouldn't be scheduled until a few months after the application was submitted. Why was an inspector snooping around?

"I'm on my way." Jason pulled the keys out of his pocket and thrust them at Kelli. "Give Pete a hand and then start on the afternoon diets. I'll be back as soon as I can."

Panic erupted on Kelli's face. She raised her palms and took a backward step. "I don't know how to help a veterinarian!"

Jason didn't have time to coddle her. He tossed the keys onto the counter with an impatient gesture. "It's a rabbit," he snapped. "It won't hurt you."

He didn't wait for an answer, but whirled and hurried out of the room. The door slammed with a resounding thud behind him.

Anger buzzed in Kelli's brain as she stared at the shut door. He didn't have to be rude. Of course she wasn't afraid of a rabbit, but she felt a lot more competent chopping yams than corralling the Easter Bunny for a vet exam.

Pete watched her from behind those enormous lenses, his cheeks rosy and his forehead slightly damp from the stuffy air in the workroom.

She forced herself to speak normally. "I'm sure you don't need a novice like me hanging around. If you want to go ahead and do whatever it is you have to do, I'll just start working on the diets, like Jason said."

"I can't go in there alone." The man looked scandalized at the idea. "Zoo rules specify that a keeper must be present at all times when a member of the veterinary staff interacts with an animal. They're very strict about that."

"I'm only an assistant keeper." Kelli let her voice drop into a confiding tone. "And between you and me, I don't have any experience working with animals."

"Then you're in luck." The man's face erupted with a smile. "I have a lot of experience."

His confidence went a long way toward putting her at ease. Pete was a veterinarian; he spent his whole life handling animals. There was nothing for her to be nervous about.

They left the workroom and wound their way through people and strollers toward the rabbit enclosure. Kelli found the key labeled Cottontails in the jumble on Jason's key ring. She unlocked the door and gestured for the vet to precede her. Once inside, he unlatched the panel and stepped right into the enclosure. The pair of rabbits scurried away to huddle beneath an outcropping, shivering with fright. Kelli remained in the closet while the veterinarian squatted on his haunches and duck-walked through the fresh straw. A small crowd gathered on the other side of the glass to watch.

"Ah, here we are." Pete beamed up at her and held a terrified bunny carefully in both hands.

"Look here, my dear. This little fellow is afraid, but other than that he appears to be entirely normal. Notice the coloring of his eyes, and the healthy layer of fat around the midsection. Now, if there was a problem, you might see ..."

With a sigh, Kelli pretended to listen attentively as the doctor warmed to his subject.

Jason walked toward the primate area as quickly as he could without breaking into a run, a thousand questions whirling through his mind. Interim inspections weren't unheard of, but usually performed only if there was cause to suspect a major problem. Even then, AZA was supposed to give some advance notice. Why was an inspector paying an unscheduled visit? Had someone filed a complaint about something? Jason clenched his jaw. Maybe AZA had gotten wind of Bob's last escape attempt. Thank goodness he'd gotten that fence repair finished.

The zoo was crowded today, he noted with distracted satisfaction. Big, fluffy clouds provided an occasional break in the heat as they floated across the blue sky, which made things pleasant for zoo goers and animals alike. He skirted the edge of the sidewalk to allow two mothers pushing a pair of orange rental strollers side-by-side to pass, then took the path to the left, toward the primates.

A wide-eyed Cameron met him in front of the capuchin enclosure. "He's over there, by the tamarins. See the guy in the green shirt?"

Jason looked in the direction Cameron indicated. A tall man in his mid-thirties stood with his feet spread apart, hands clasped behind his back, studying the black-and-white primates intently. He didn't look familiar. "Did he introduce himself?"

Cameron, a young, slightly built guy who'd joined Cougar Bay last year, shook his head. "I recognize him from when we went through the AZA inspection in my last job, when I was interning up in Georgia. I'm sure it's the same guy." Worry colored the kid's tone. "What do you think he's doing here?"

Since the accreditation application consisted of an extensive amount of documentation that touched literally every area of the zoo, all the employees were involved. Everyone knew the status of the project and that an unannounced inspection six weeks before the submission deadline was cause for concern.

Jason shrugged. "I don't know, but I'm going to find out."

Cameron hung back while Jason strode toward the inspector. He dodged a pair of laughing girls as they ran to the capuchins, and came to a stop beside the green-clad man.

"Hello." Jason schooled any hint of anxiety from his tone and stuck out a hand. "I'm Jason Andover, the interim director here at Cougar Bay."

The man looked startled for a moment, then a smile broke out on his face as he shook Jason's hand with a firm grip. "Cliff

Reiker. Nice to meet you. I see I've been identified, though I can't imagine how. I've never been here before today."

Jason replied in the same easy tone. "One of my keepers spotted you and remembered you from a previous job."

The man's gaze strayed behind Jason's left shoulder, where Cameron no doubt stood watching. "Ah. I had no idea I had such a recognizable face." His eyes shifted back to Jason. "I take it I've caused a stir."

"Well, naturally we're curious why an AZA inspector would show up unannounced." Jason shoved his hand in his pocket. "I hope nothing's wrong."

"No, not at all," the man hurried to say. "I'm in Florida on vacation with my family. The wife and I have spent all week doing the theme-park thing, and we're heading back home tomorrow. But I couldn't resist checking out the zoo while I was here."

A sheepish smile curled his lips. The tension evaporated from Jason's shoulders. The man loved zoos, like everyone else in the industry. Jason didn't travel often, but wherever he went, he made time to visit any zoo in the area, especially if he'd never been there before. This guy was just doing the same.

"Well, Cougar Bay isn't the biggest zoo around, but we're pretty proud of our collection."

"You should be." Cliff's head moved as he looked toward the row of animal exhibits lining the path around them. "Your animals all look in fine shape. I'm a primate man myself, and that orang is a beauty."

Jason's chest swelled. "She is, isn't she? Cocoa's one of the local favorites."

A pair of kids raced toward them shouting, "Daddy, there you are!" The girl threw her arms around Cliff's waist, while the boy bounced on the toes of his sneakers with enthusiasm. "They have a lion, Dad! You should see him. And some cougars and a bobcat."

An attractive woman approached, and Cliff placed an arm around her waist as he introduced her to Jason. "My wife, Marge."

Jason shook her hand. "Nice to meet you."

"Jason is the interim zoo director." Cliff's expression grew solemn. "I read about the previous director's death in the paper the other day. Sad news."

Jason nodded. "She'll be missed."

"Honey, the kids want to go see the meerkats," Marge said. "Are you coming with us, or are you going to hang out here all day?" She gave him a playful shove and told Jason, "Put him in front of a cage full of monkeys and you have to pry him away with a crowbar."

Jason laughed. "Actually, we have a half-dozen squirrel monkeys in the Small Animal building, right next to the meerkats. I was just heading over there myself."

"Terrific," Cliff said. "We'll join you."

Jason led them in the direction he'd just come. While the kids ran ahead, he and Cliff compared zoo experiences as they walked. They discovered some common friends, not at all unusual in the zoo community.

A moment before they turned a corner on the sidewalk that took them into view of the Small Animal building, Jason knew something was wrong. High-pitched shrieks filled the air, not the typical noise of playful children. These sounded more like squeals of alarm. *Oh, no. Has something happened to Kelli?* He sprinted ahead, Cliff a half step behind him. They dodged through a crowd of children and parents exiting the building at a run.

They dashed through the doorway as the last of the occupants ran out, and Jason skidded to a halt just inside. Kelli stood a few feet away, her arms wrapped tightly around her middle, hugging herself. She turned, her round eyes full moons of distress.

"I forgot to close the door. I didn't mean for him to get out."

That's when Jason noticed movement at the other end of the building. A skunk ran along the floor, its black and white body swaying with a distinctive waddle, bushy tail thrust straight up in the air. It reached the far wall, turned and ran halfway down the hall in their direction. When it caught sight of them, it turned again to race away. The poor animal was clearly terrified.

He stepped in front of Kelli. "Where's Pete?" He didn't mean to snap, but she winced at his tone.

"He—he left after he examined the rabbit. I—" She gulped. "I did the skunk's lunch and figured I'd go ahead and feed it."

Jason's hands balled into fists, but he managed to keep his tone even. "You never, ever, unlock an animal's enclosure with the outside door open."

Her head drooped forward until her chin touched her chest. "I'm sorry. I forgot."

Cliff, whose expression was no longer friendly, stepped forward to insert himself into the conversation. "Don't you have clearly outlined shift procedures, Andover?"

Andover. A minute ago it was *Jason.*

"Of course we do. She just started this morning, so she hasn't been fully trained yet."

His eyebrows arched. "You left these animals in the care of someone who wasn't fully trained?"

Now it was Jason's turn to wince. He'd left Kelli with Pete, a fully trained veterinarian, and with instructions to do diets when Pete left. Given her aversion to animals, he never dreamed she'd try to enter an enclosure alone.

But he shouldn't have left his keys with her. *My mistake. And it's a big one.*

If he listed a bunch of excuses, like the fact that they were short-handed, he'd only make things worse. Instead he clamped his mouth shut and strode toward the open door beside the skunk enclosure. Inside, he retrieved the small pet crate they used as Felix's shift. The poor animal was so frightened he ran inside as soon as Jason set it on the floor and opened the door.

When Felix was safely back in his enclosure and huddled in the security of his den, Jason rejoined Kelli and Cliff. They had not moved from just inside the building's entrance. Kelli still hugged herself tightly, her cheeks stained with a miserable red flush. Cliff stood with his arms folded across his chest.

"I'm sorry," Kelli repeated as he approached. "I should have just—"

Jason cut her off with a raised hand. "It's my fault. My responsibility."

He almost added, "No harm done," but when he risked a glance into Cliff's stern face, the words died on his lips. He had the sinking feeling harm had, indeed, been done. They had not heard the last of this incident.

Chapter Eight

"What made you decide to go ahead and feed Felix without me?"

Even though his voice no longer held that angry tone, Kelli couldn't look into Jason's face. She focused instead on chopping an apple into small pieces for the squirrel monkeys.

"His banana slices were starting to brown, and I thought it'd be better if his food was fresh when he got it." She swallowed and scooped apple into the bowl on the scale. "He went into his crate so easily for you, I figured he'd do the same for me."

No need to mention that she'd been trying to prove a point to Jason. Caring for animals wasn't brain surgery; she could do it easily, if she wanted to. It was a matter of choice that had kept her away from animals for almost twenty years. Not lack of ability, and certainly not fear.

Well, maybe a *little* fear, but that was entirely understandable, given her childhood experience with the lion. Even her therapist said so. And that was none of Jason's business.

"Shifting isn't a trick the animals do, like sitting or rolling over. True, it's part of the training we do with every animal at the zoo, but they do it because they trust the person asking them to shift. That's part of the special relationship a keeper has with an animal in his or her care."

"So you're saying the reason that skunk escaped is because he didn't trust me?" Sheer willpower kept her from rolling her eyes.

"Yes. That, and the fact that you left the external door open."

She ducked her head and sliced off a chunk of orange. He had stressed the importance of closing the door first thing this morning. A dumb mistake on her part, no doubt about it, but she'd already apologized once. She wasn't about to keep doing it. Instead, she hacked the orange into small pieces with vicious jabs and grumbled, "I never thought I'd be trying to earn the trust of a skunk."

He rubbed his eyes with a thumb and forefinger. "You probably won't, not with that attitude."

She turned to look at him straight on. "What is that supposed to mean?"

His eyebrows rose as he stared at the knife in her hand. Heat suffused her face as she realized she was holding it like a weapon, the business end pointed toward Jason's stomach. Hurriedly, she turned back to the counter.

"I only meant that animals have a kind of sixth sense. They can tell when someone doesn't like them, and they tend to avoid those people."

Good. Fine by her if the animals all avoided her. That would make the next six months easier. She could chop their food and clean their cages and let someone else worry about feeding the wretched things.

She remembered a question she'd wanted to ask. "Who was that guy, the mean-looking one who came back with you?"

Jason closed his eyes and groaned. "That was an AZA inspector. Just about the worst person in the world to witness a lapse in security. Our accreditation review is coming up in a couple of months, and he is sure to report this incident."

"I take it that's a bad thing."

"Oh, yeah. See, Cougar Bay doesn't actually own these animals. All zoo animals are owned by the AZA, and they pretty much determine everything about them. Which ones are bred, where they're housed. They make sure everything is done in the best interest of the species."

Kelli's jaw dropped open. "You mean they could just decide they want to move Baya and Gasira somewhere else?"

"If they did, they'd have good reasons, probably related to their environment or safety." He shook his head miserably. "I didn't make a good impression on Cliff Reiker today, that's for sure."

Kelli felt awful. She may not like the silly animals, but she wouldn't knowingly do anything to harm them or cause them to be sent away. "But you didn't do anything wrong. You weren't even here. Surely he knows that."

Jason heaved a loud sigh. "No, it was my mistake, one of several I've made this morning." He straightened and gave her a grim smile. "But we're going to set that right, beginning now. When we finish up here, I'm taking you back to the office and sitting you down in front of those training videos. And after that, I've got five binders' worth of procedures you can read through."

She groaned. The only thing she could imagine worse than cleaning out animal cages was reading about it.

Kelli leaned back from her mother's desk and rubbed her eyes. She still had several client accounts to close out before the end of the month, but the figures on her laptop were starting to blur, which meant it was time to stop for the night. She glanced at her watch. Correction. One a.m. no longer counted as night. She'd better get some sleep.

The entire afternoon had been spent watching videos of keepers working with animals, demonstrating the proper way to approach, shift, feed, train, examine and interact in every way with most of the species at Cougar Bay. Not professional-quality videos, but not bad either. The instructors on the recordings wore Cougar Bay uniforms, and Kelli vaguely recognized several of them. Even Jason had put in an appearance, looking a few years younger than now, his hair a touch longer but still alarmingly handsome in a rugged, outdoorsy way. She'd had a hard time focusing on his instructions. He looked directly into the camera as he spoke, and more than once Kelli had found herself returning his infectious smile, her thoughts straying to the moments they'd spent crammed into the dark closets of the Small Animal building together.

But then she saw someone she didn't expect, and thoughts of Jason had fled. The first time Lillian stepped in front of the camera, she'd felt as though someone punched her in the stomach.

Jason could have warned me about that.

But after a few minutes, Kelli had almost forgotten she was watching her mom. Lillian was every inch the professional zoo director. She took the same clinical, no-nonsense approach to instructing new employees on zoo procedure that she'd displayed during her infrequent phone calls with her daughter. The only difference Kelli could detect was a softening in her voice when she addressed the animals directly.

When she got to the section on care for the big cats, Kelli had hit the fast-forward button.

A movement at the office door drew Kelli's attention. Leo had become brave enough to risk an appearance. The cat sat in the hallway and watched her with an unblinking stare. Kelli returned his gaze for a moment, then placed her palms on the desk and slowly started to rise. At the first sign of movement, Leo dashed away toward his closet.

"You don't trust me, do you, cat? Well, you're in good company. The skunk doesn't like me either."

What would Dr. Reynolds have made of that? Would he have said the animals' distrust was because Kelli was sending off signals that she was untrustworthy? The same way he claimed she broadcast signals to men that she wasn't lovable?

Jason's angry face when he'd first seen the skunk running down the hallway loomed in her mind's eye.

With a savage gesture, Kelli shut down the computer. She was too tired to think about Jason. Or Dr. Reynolds and their final, irritating therapy session last year. Giving in to a wide yawn as she left the office, she checked the lock on the front door, then crossed to the back and stood looking through the window. The sloping yard was bathed in white light. Not a thing moved. On impulse, she stepped outside. The light from the living room illuminated part of the covered porch. She stepped out into the patchy grass. An impossibly huge full moon hung in a starry sky.

"I'm not unlovable, am I, Lord?" Her whisper, directed toward the heavens, seemed to float upward and disappear in the cool night air. "You love me."

That was one certainty Kelli had learned to cling to, that God loved her. And Nana loved her, too. Who else mattered?

An image of green-brown eyes in a warmly tanned face rose unbidden before her. Jason didn't even think she could earn the trust of a skunk. Did that mean she couldn't earn his trust either? A longing stirred deep inside, almost undetectable. She pushed it away. Trust was a two-way street, one she was determined to steer clear of when it came to Jason Andover.

But an unsettling thought plagued her tired mind. Dr. Reynolds had said much the same thing as Jason in that last session. His words had sent Kelli storming out of his office, vowing never to return. The fact was, Kelli wasn't capable of forming permanent attachments. She repelled men like the wrong end of a magnet.

There must be something wrong with me. My own mother sent me away. Why should I expect any guy to want me around?

Which was dumb, she knew in her rational mind. But her heart had never been rational.

An eerie sound from the direction of the zoo rose into the air, a long, suspended howl that swelled in pitch and sent shivers coursing down her spine. A few seconds later, another howl chimed in, and a third, until a chorus of uncanny cries filled the night. With a shudder, Kelli retreated to the house and locked the door behind her.

Jason stood at the corner of the kangaroo yard, staring up at the faint glow visible above the privacy fence. The light, he knew, came from Lil's house. He'd seen it many times before as he made his late-night rounds of the zoo grounds. Seemed Kelli was a workaholic, just like her mom. Just like him.

A lone wolf howl floated on the misty darkness, the sound joined by others to create a community song that modulated in tone and harmonics. Jason smiled. Bob was doing his thing, leading his pack in the activity that many believed strengthened the social bond between packmates.

The glow above the fence winked out. Jason pushed the button on his watch to illuminate the face. He had to get up in five hours; time to head home. With a sigh, Jason turned toward the zoo entrance. He flipped on his flashlight and aimed the beam back and forth as he assured himself that everything was as it should be. Glowing eyes of different sizes blinked back at him as he walked.

Only everything was not as it should be, hadn't been since he laid eyes on Kelli Jackson at the memorial service yesterday morning. Conflict raged inside him. That she carried deep wounds was obvious to anyone who spent more than a few minutes with her. She walked through the zoo grounds with tense muscles, as though surrounded by deadly enemies, her fight-or-flight instincts on high alert. Animals picked that up instinctively, so it was no surprise Felix had tried to escape from her.

His biggest mistake of the day hadn't been merely in plunging her into animal care without first showing her the training videos. It had been in wanting so badly to show her how charming the animals were. He'd made the mistake of thinking if she interacted with the most harmless of the zoo's collection right up front, he could win her over.

Lesson learned. Kelli's trust was going to be even harder to win than the exotic animals he'd dealt with his entire career.

Lil, turns out your daughter is just as hard-headed as you. Whatever those fears are you want her to face, they're pretty ingrained. It's not going to be easy.

He stopped on the path as a thought struck him. If he succeeded in helping Kelli overcome her fears, he would accomplish the task he promised Lil he'd undertake. If he failed to do that, he would still succeed in gaining a huge boost for the zoo's expansion project. Kind of funny that he'd win either way.

Of course, a glass-half-empty man would say that meant he'd lose either way, too.

Both results shared a common outcome: Kelli would return to Denver. A surprising wave of sadness lapped gently across the shores of his mind. He thrust it away and focused instead on the task at hand. The flashlight beam swept the peccary pen until he located the pair of occupants snoozing deeply in the far corner. Jason snapped off the light and headed for the zoo exit.

Sometimes he thought life would have been less complicated if he'd become a brain surgeon instead of a zookeeper.

Chapter Nine

On Sunday morning Kelli drove Lillian's car to Redeemer Community Church for the eleven o'clock service. She'd passed the church on her way to the grocery store Saturday, after a long, dull day spent reading zoo procedures from giant three-ring binders. The marquee out front displayed the same sort of pithy saying her minister in Denver might select. *HELP IS JUST A PRAYER AWAY.* Kelli figured she could use all the help she could get.

The first person she saw when she walked through the door was Jason Andover.

Kelli stopped short. He stood in the doorway to the sanctuary, talking to a stout elderly woman. *He hasn't seen me yet. If I leave now—*

But in the next instant, he looked up, and their eyes locked over the top of the woman's satiny red hat. He said something to excuse himself and then crossed the distance between them.

"Kelli, what a surprise."

For a moment she thought he might sweep her into a hug by way of greeting, but he stopped just in front of her and, after an awkward half second, shoved his hands into his pants pockets.

"What are you doing here?"

Not exactly the standard greeting for a first-time visitor. She raised her eyebrows.

He must have realized how odd his question sounded because he hurried on. "I mean, I didn't know you went to church. If I had, I would have invited you to join us."

"Us?" The question shot out faster than she intended, and Kelli looked down, embarrassed. Did he have a wife or a girl-friend? She wouldn't want to intrude.

"My mother and I." He turned as a group of adults filed down one of the side hallways and into the sanctuary. "There's her Sunday school class now. Come on. I'll introduce you."

Kelli followed him toward the sanctuary, her step lighter than a moment before. Although she probably wouldn't have accepted his invitation, she couldn't very well get out of it now, could she? Besides, given the choice, she preferred to sit with someone, even her new boss. Sitting alone felt too much like being the loner at the middle-school lunch table.

Jason intercepted a woman heading toward the sanctuary and pulled her aside with a hand through her arm. She turned, and Kelli couldn't help returning her generous smile.

"Kelli Jackson, this is my mother, Barb Andover." He paused, then added, "Mom, Kelli is my late boss's daughter."

Her hand felt warm as she grasped Kelli's. Solicitude flooded the eyes that looked into hers, the same green-brown as Jason's.

"Oh, my dear, I'm so sorry for your loss." She covered their clasped hands with her other one and squeezed.

"Thank you." Kelli lowered her gaze to the floor, unable to withstand the deep compassion she saw in Mrs. Andover's expression. The woman wore a look of shared sorrow, one that could only come from an intimate knowledge of the emotion. Jason's mother had lost someone close, and the grief was still fresh. Her own mother, maybe? Or, because she appeared to be alone, maybe her husband? Kelli stole a quick look at Jason. Had he lost a family member recently?

"We'd better get a seat." Jason put a hand on his mother's arm to guide her into the sanctuary, his smile inviting Kelli to join them.

Kelli fell in beside him, conscious of the curious gazes fixed on her as they made their way to an empty row of chairs halfway down the center aisle. She seated herself beside Jason and looked around. Several people nodded politely and she returned the gesture, then caught sight of another familiar face. Reverend Stephens, the minister from Lillian's memorial service, was seated up on the podium reading from a Bible.

She leaned sideways and whispered a question to Jason. "Did my mother go to church here?"

"Occasionally." His lips twisted with a wry smile. "Mostly on special occasions, like Christmas and Easter, until six months ago."

Six months ago. *When she found out she had cancer.*

Kelli nodded. Lillian had sought solace in God during her final days. With the knowledge came a sense of relief, and Kelli leaned against the padded seat back, her gaze fixed on the huge cross behind Reverend Stephens. *At least she had spiritual comfort, even though she didn't have any family support.*

Not my fault, Kelli reminded herself. *If she'd told me, I would have helped.* She shifted sideways in the seat. *Somehow.*

On the other side of Jason, Mrs. Andover leaned forward. "Kelli, how long will you be staying in Florida?"

Kelli glanced at Jason. Had he told his mother of the contents of Lillian's trust? Judging from her guileless expression, apparently not. How in the world would she explain this bizarre, and temporary, move to Florida? She stared without answering, her mind blank, until Jason came to her rescue.

"Kelli's taken a job at the zoo for a while. She'll be here indefinitely."

Surprise colored the woman's features, which she politely masked almost as soon as it appeared. "How nice. We'll have to get together. Our ladies' Bible study on Wednesday nights is mostly older women, but we'd love to have you join us."

Kelli was saved from replying when a handful of musicians trooped down the aisle and went to a corner of the platform where a variety of instruments lay ready, signaling the beginning of the service. The minister stood and stepped up to the podium.

Jason leaned sideways. His whisper tickled her cheek with warm, mint-flavored breath. "If you know what's good for you, you'll stay away from the Wednesday-night ladies' group. Nice as they can be, but they're a bunch of matchmakers. Their children, grandchildren, neighbors—any single person between the ages of eighteen and thirty-five is considered fair game. A beautiful woman like you would be irresistible to them."

His grin, meant no doubt to be conspiratorial, sent Kelli's pulse into a thudding tempo. She barely heard the minister's introductory remarks through her whirling thoughts.

He thinks I'm beautiful.

By the time the service ended, Kelli had regained her composure. The minister's sermon went mostly unheeded, but she was able to file out of the church at Jason's side without his compliment echoing in her brain. She even managed to exchange a few pleasant words with Reverend Stephens at the door.

Outside in the oppressive heat, she veered toward her car. A voice from behind stopped her.

"Kelli, wait a minute."

She turned to find Jason and his mother hurrying to catch up with her.

"We were wondering—That is, my mom wondered—" A flush hovered beneath Jason's tanned cheeks.

Mrs. Andover gave him a disdainful look before turning a smile on Kelli. "Would you like to join us for brunch, dear?

There's a nice restaurant not far from here where we go whenever Jason doesn't have to rush off to work."

Kelli didn't hesitate to decline. During the service she'd come to a realization. She may be stuck at the zoo for six months, but that didn't mean she was going to fall at the feet of her mother's handpicked replacement, no matter how he flattered her. For all she knew, his earlier compliment was merely a ruse, an attempt to win her trust. She must never forget what Jason's precious zoo stood to gain if she let her guard down. Certainly he wouldn't forget it.

She poured regret into her voice. "Thank you for the offer, but I'm afraid I've got some work to do this afternoon myself."

"Oh." Mrs. Andover's expression fell, then brightened a moment later. "Well, next week, perhaps. And don't forget about Wednesday night."

"That reminds me." Kelli looked at Jason. She hated having to ask his permission, but he *was* her boss now. "My return flight to Denver is Wednesday morning. If it's okay with you, I'd like to go ahead and keep that flight. I've got some things to take care of at my place and my grandmother's before we close them up for six months."

His eyebrows arched. "Your grandmother's?"

Kelli nodded. "I can't leave her in Denver alone for that long. She's coming out here to stay with me."

"Well, the first Sunday you're back, plan on going to brunch with us," Mrs. Andover said. "Your grandmother, too."

Kelli smiled her thanks without committing. She started to turn away, but Jason stopped her with a hand on her arm.

He peered intently into her eyes, as though trying to read her thoughts. "You are coming back, aren't you?"

Breathlessness threatened. Kelli forced herself to reply lightly. "Of course. You can't get rid of me that easily."

A slow smile transformed his lips. "Good," he said, his voice low.

Swallowing against a dry throat, Kelli turned away. For a moment there, it looked like Jason really thought she'd leave and not return. But instead of the triumph she would have expected, he'd looked almost sad.

Jason watched her walk away. He didn't move as she slid into Lil's old Toyota, backed out of the parking place and disappeared around the corner of the church.

Then he became aware of his mother watching him with a knowing smile.

"She's a pretty girl," Mom commented.

Uh-oh. The matchmaking antennas were twitching like an insect on high alert.

He answered with a noncommittal "Hmm" as he steered her toward his car.

"What was that she said about six months?"

Jason dug the keys out of his pocket and punched the Unlock button. "Kelli's only working at the zoo on a temporary basis. It was a request from her mother."

He didn't want to go into the whole thing about the trust with anyone, even Mom. It felt like a breach of Lil's privacy. And Kelli's.

"And then she'll go back to Denver?"

Jason opened the car door and held his mother's arm while she sat down. "That's right," he told her before he closed the door.

He swallowed a sigh as he rounded the front of the car. No doubt he was in for a grilling at the restaurant. He halfway wished he could come up with an excuse to skip their Sunday ritual and take her straight home. But he didn't have the heart to do that to her. Mom was so lonely since Dad died, and Jason knew how much she looked forward to the time they spent together. As did he. If only Kelli had agreed to join them.

He paused, his hand on the door handle. Having her beside him in church felt amazingly ... normal. Like she belonged there. Did she notice how her husky alto voice had blended with his as they sang? Or the way his skin buzzed, almost vibrated, when he touched her smooth arm a moment ago?

Apparently not. She'd sure left in a hurry.

That's for the best. In fact, it would probably be best if she found another church to attend while she was in town. He was her boss, after all, and besides, the specter of his failure with Aimee still loomed painfully. And would for many years to come.

But I'm different now. I've grown up. I'm responsible. A Believer. God forgave me, washed me clean, like the preacher says.

That may be so, but Jason knew he'd messed up royally with Aimee and he had no reason to believe he wouldn't do the same with Kelli or any other woman. Besides, he had too much going on in his life right now to worry about women.

Except the one he was taking to brunch. He opened the door and slid into the car.

Chapter Ten

On Monday morning, Kelli expected to be stuck in the conference room again, parked behind another stack of training manuals or something. Instead, she entered the office to find Jason standing beside Angela's desk, waiting for her.

"I have a board meeting to get ready for today, so this morning you get to work with Raul." Jason's tone wouldn't have been any different if he'd just announced that today was her execution day.

Angela awarded her a sympathetic grimace. "Don't let him get to you, Kelli. He's grouchy, but down deep he's really a nice guy."

Kelli tilted her head and eyed them with caution. "Raul's the one who sprained his ankle?"

Jason nodded. "He's back, but he's on crutches and needs some help." He lowered his voice and mumbled something that sounded like, "Whether he wants it or not."

She didn't have time to react before Jason opened the door and gestured for her to precede him. With a farewell shrug for Angela, she left and then walked fast to keep up with the long-legged pace he set.

"So I take it Raul doesn't play well with others?"

Jason acknowledged her wit with a chuckle. "You could say that. He's been here a million years, so he feels like he owns the place, especially the Small Animal building." He cocked his head to look sideways at her. "Lil was one of the few people he actually liked. Maybe he'll cut you some slack because you're her daughter."

They passed a small yard on the left with a couple of strange pig-looking things inside, both of them wallowing on the ground in a cloud of dust. Kelli held her breath until they were well past, partly so she wouldn't breath in the dust and partly because they smelled horrible.

"You'll work with Raul this morning," Jason told her as they approached the Small Animal building, "and then with Cameron this afternoon."

Kelli studied him through narrowed eyes. "What kind of animals does Cameron work with?"

"Primates."

She heaved a relieved sigh. She could handle a few monkeys.

When they approached the building, Jason started to open the door, then paused with his hand on the handle. Kelli had to tilt her head to look into his face.

"If you want me to keep an eye on the house while you're gone, I'll be happy to do that."

"Thank you. Somebody needs to feed the cat." She twisted her lips. "Maybe you can get him to leave the closet. I sure can't."

"Give him time. Leo just takes a while to warm up to people." His tone became softer, more personal than a moment before, the drawl more pronounced. "I hope you were serious about coming back."

Mouth dry, Kelli cast about for a response. Was he asking as her boss or as Lillian's trustee? Or was his comment more personal? The soft look in his eyes would have been flirting in any other man. And the pounding in her chest would have meant she liked it.

She tore her gaze away from his face and spoke to the hand resting on the door. "I was serious."

A smile played around his lips for a moment, then he swung the door outward and held it while she entered.

Raul stood peering into the desert-fox enclosure, balanced on metal crutches, his right foot in a blue medical boot. He looked up, turned and hobbled toward them with surprising speed. One look at his wizened face sent uneasiness shafting through Kelli.

"I don't need no helper," he announced halfway down the hall. "I can handle my animals fine by m'self."

Kelli shrank under the glare he turned on her, but Jason stood firm. He acted as if the man had not spoken.

"Kelli Jackson, meet Raul Santos. Raul has been at Cougar Bay longer than anyone else on staff."

From his name, Kelli had expected someone of Hispanic origin. The dark hue of his skin might have been hereditary, or it might have come from a lifetime spent working in the sun. Hard to tell behind all the creases and wrinkles.

Scraggly gray eyebrows dropped low over piercing dark eyes. "Been here at this zoo since I was twelve years old, and I don't need no help from no green gal who ain't got the smarts to close the door behind her."

Kelli winced. Apparently word of Friday's incident had made the rounds. *So much for him cutting me some slack because of my mother.*

Jason spoke in a placating tone. "That's exactly why I want her to work with you, Raul. She needs someone who knows what's what to show her the ropes. With your extensive experience, you're the best man for the job."

Raul wasn't falling for the flattery. The glare he turned on Jason would have flattened most men. Kelli's opinion of Jason rose when he not only didn't flare up, but actually smiled into Raul's scowling face.

"Besides," he continued, "you're going to have trouble getting down on the floor to clean those exhibits properly. I don't have to tell you, of all people, how important cleanliness is to the animals' health. Kelli can help you. She did a good job with that Friday."

Raul turned a skeptical frown on her, as though he didn't think her capable of adequately cleaning a cage. She clamped her teeth together to keep from snapping a sarcastic comment, which certainly wouldn't help. She was just about to suggest to Jason that she could go work with the monkeys this morning instead of waiting until after lunch when Raul yielded.

"I'll check her work," he told Jason, as though she were not standing right beside him. "If she don't do it right, I'll make her do it again."

While Kelli fumed, Jason clapped the man on the arm. "She'll do fine. At noon send her over to Cameron."

As he turned away, he gave Kelli an apologetic smile and a one-shouldered shrug. Then he was gone.

Kelli watched the door close behind him, dismayed to feel so forlorn at his departure. She turned warily to face her grouchy taskmaster.

"First things first," Raul told her. "I don't care who your mama was. You're my assistant. That means you hafta do whatever I tell you, y'hear?"

For a moment, Kelli bristled. She drew upright, spine stiff. Her, an assistant to this cantankerous old man? Then she happened to look down at the animal on the other side of the window beside them. It was Felix, the skunk. Her indignation dissolved.

"I hear you." She forced a brave smile. "Where do we start?"

By noon, Kelli had to admit that Raul knew what he was doing. He may not get along with people, but he seemed to have a special bond with his animals. When he walked down the hallway, every animal ran to the front of its enclosure to watch him pass. Even though he wouldn't allow Kelli to come into the closet with him while they shifted—which was actually a relief—she heard him crooning to them in their shifts as she scrubbed their homes clean.

He wasn't much on explanations, but seemed to delight in barking orders and snapping sarcastically if she didn't perform exactly as he expected. The yam pieces had to be *just so* for the cavies, the carrots exactly the right size for the porcupines. He measured the vitamin powder with precision, and Kelli didn't mention Jason's eyeball approach.

She was a little dismayed that he wouldn't let her hand-feed Baya and Gasira, as Jason had. She sort of wanted to see if they would remember her from Friday. Her disappointment that Raul refused to allow her any contact with them surprised her, but she shrugged it off. She was putting in time, that's all. What difference did it make if the animals never knew who she was?

Her last job before Raul released her was to feed the meerkats their afternoon snack. When they'd been transferred into their crates, Raul stood outside the enclosure, watching her every movement through the glass and snapping directions.

"Scatter a few of those mealworms on the rocks."

Kelli obediently sprinkled some of the carefully counted worms from the bowl onto the fabricated boulders inside the meerkats' enclosure.

"Not that many," Raul barked. "Save a few."

Biting back a retort. Kelli picked up half of the worms and put them back in the bowl. Funny, but they no longer made her flesh crawl. Who would have thought she'd grow accustomed to handling worms so quickly?

"What about the rest of them?" She held the bowl up to the glass for Raul's inspection.

"Bury 'em."

Kelli raised her eyebrows. "Excuse me?"

"Right there." Raul stabbed a finger toward the sand-covered floor in front of his position. "Dig a hole and bury 'em. Then mound up the sand over top, so they'll know where to look."

With a shrug, Kelli did as instructed. When she finished, she took Raul's place in the hall while he released the meerkats into their home. Then he joined her to watch as they scampered toward the worms on the rocks and gobbled them up.

"Jason didn't have me bury worms Friday," she commented, her eyes fixed on the furry animals.

"Jason don't know everything, does he?" His wrinkled lips pursed sideways. "It's good for 'em to make 'em work for their food, like they would in the wild."

That made sense. The meerkats finished off all the worms out in the open. Kelli watched them scurry around, checking for any they might have missed.

"They're not digging for the buried ones." She turned a worried look on Raul. "Maybe I didn't do it right."

He seemed unconcerned. "Just wait."

Sure enough, after a few minutes, one meerkat sprinted over to the mounded sand. He leaned forward and started digging with surprising speed. His front paws were a blur of activity as sand flew in all directions. He uncovered a worm, darted forward to scoop it up with his mouth and kept digging even as he swallowed.

Kelli laughed out loud. With the blackened mask around his eyes, he looked like a child playing bandit and digging for buried treasure.

Raul actually slapped her on the back and displayed the first smile she'd seen from him all morning. "There, see? You did just fine."

Kelli straightened her shoulders. Something told her Raul didn't give praise often.

"So," she said, glancing at her watch, "I guess I'd better go help the primate guy. Unless you have something else you need me to do."

"Nah, you go on."

He didn't take his eyes off the meerkats, but Kelli sensed he had something else to say, so she waited. Finally, he spoke without looking at her.

"You can come back and help me tomorrow, if you want."

She didn't bother to hold back her smile. "Thanks. I'd like that."

When Kelli left the building, the sun seemed to shine brighter than it had since she'd arrived in Florida.

Jason plucked at his tie and wished he could take off the uncomfortable thing. A glance around the room revealed that he could have opted for something less formal, because most of the board members were dressed casually. Too late now. His collared white shirt would gape open and look unprofessional without the noose to hold it in place.

The surroundings themselves were enough to set a man's knees knocking. Why the board elected to pay for a fancy downtown hotel meeting room instead of the zoo's conference room made no sense to Jason. Seemed like a colossal waste of money to him, but what did he know? He was just a zookeeper, not a high-powered executive.

Kelli would probably feel right at home here.

Because she was an accountant, no doubt she was accustomed to meetings and presentations and all that. In fact, she'd made no secret of the fact that she felt more comfortable in an office environment than she ever would in a zoo.

I wish she were here right now.

The thought came out of nowhere and brought with it a lingering sense of dismay. Thoughts of Kelli were starting to intrude on him at odd times. And this was certainly one of the oddest. He didn't have time to think about her right now.

He shuffled the papers on the table in front of him, mostly to give his hands something to do.

The door opened and the quiet conversations around the room went silent as a woman entered. Jason recognized her as Francine Cowell, the most recently appointed board member. Lil had taken her on a tour of the zoo last year and introduced them. Jason couldn't remember what she did for a day job. Something to do with real estate, maybe.

"Sorry I'm late." Mrs. Cowell flashed an apologetic smile around the table and slipped into an empty chair near the door.

At the head of the table, Daniel Lewis glanced at his watch and addressed the room. "Let's get started. I'm hoping we can wrap this up by four-thirty. I have to meet with a client across town at six." Nods around the table. "Our first order of business is the official appointment of the new zoo director."

All eyes turned toward Jason. He resisted the urge to tug at his tie again.

"I hope you've all had an opportunity to read the documentation I forwarded last week about Ms. Mitchell's testamentary trust, and her letter of recommendation for Mr. Andover. Plus, I think I've spoken with each of you personally. But for the official record, allow me to summarize."

Lewis glanced at the woman seated next to him. He'd introduced her to Jason earlier as his assistant who would be taking the official minutes of the board meeting. Her fingers flew over the keyboard of a miniature laptop as Lewis spoke, outlining the provisions of Lil's trust. When he stated the condition regarding the appointment of the new director, heat threatened to rise into Jason's face. He caught Mrs. Cowell's encouraging smile across the table.

Lewis ended his recitation with, "Does anyone have any questions or comments?"

Midway down the table, Robert Young leaned forward. He was a banker by profession and had been on the zoo's board of directors for longer than Jason had been employed there.

He fixed Jason with a stern look. "I received a call from an acquaintance at AZA this morning, describing an alarming incident that occurred last week involving a breach in animal handling procedures."

Jason fought to hold back a groan. Cliff Reiker had wasted no time after returning from his vacation.

He swallowed. "We did have an incident Friday, and an AZA inspector was on hand to witness it." Jason managed to keep his tone even as he described the event, downplaying Kelli's part in it. He didn't stop to think why he preferred not to have the board think badly of her. He ended by saying, "I take full responsibility for the lapse in standard procedure and I can promise you, it *will not* happen again."

He held the gaze of every board member, letting them see his sincerity. He saw a few encouraging nods, but also a couple of scowls.

Lewis, his face impassive, addressed Mr. Young. "Did your contact at AZA indicate whether they're planning to take further action?"

Young shook his head. "They may let it drop, now that he's reported the incident to us. Or they may file some sort of formal report."

The man next to him asked, "Will this affect Cougar Bay's accreditation?"

"Not necessarily." Young peered at Jason. "Not unless they schedule an interim inspection and find something else wrong."

"They won't." Jason spoke with more confidence than he felt. True, Cougar Bay followed all the rules—usually—but when you were dealing with exotic animals, unexpected things happened.

Mrs. Cowell tapped her pen on the paper in front of her. "I'm sure that incident was a one-time thing. Personally, I see no reason not to honor Lil's request and confirm Jason as zoo director."

"Especially given the, ah, benefits of his appointment." The man to Jason's right caught his eye and gave an apologetic shrug. "Not that you wouldn't make a fine director without the $700,000 bonus."

"The money's designated," Lewis reminded them. "We can't just spend it however we want."

"But the African Habitat is a good thing for the zoo." Mrs. Cowell's voice rose at the end, as though asking a question.

Lewis nodded. "That's true, but an expansion project of that magnitude will take a lot more than $700,000."

Young gave a quiet cough. "Of course, if Lil's daughter doesn't perform up to par, we'll have a much better start on the project. With over a million dollars down, we'll have no problem getting the bank to fund the rest." Young leaned forward and caught Jason's eye. "Any chance that will happen?"

Jason's hands went clammy. Was there more to the question than appeared? Was Mr. Young asking if Jason could affect the outcome of Kelli's performance? He dropped his hands in his lap and rubbed them on his trousers.

"She seems determined to stick it out," he answered.

"Yes, but she's already messed up once, in a big way."

Jason squared his shoulders. "I've already said, that was my fault."

Young's eyes narrowed. Jason had a hard time not looking away. Did he think Jason was protecting Kelli unduly?

Was he?

Finally, Young spoke. "If she does something that endangers our standing as an AZA-accredited facility, I'd say that's a pretty clear indication of poor performance. The money wouldn't even be a consideration." His stare became hard. "Wouldn't you agree, Andover?"

An awkward silence settled in the room as they all waited for Jason to answer. And what could he say? Kelli might still decide to leave on her own. If she didn't, Jason would absolutely refuse to do anything to force her out, if that's what Young was trying to get at. But if she did something to mess up the zoo's accreditation process, he'd have to treat her just like any other keeper.

Only, the other keepers all had years of training and experience. Kelli had none. The possibility of her making a mistake was exponentially greater.

I'll just have to make sure she doesn't.

He squared his shoulders. "Of course."

After a moment, Young nodded.

Lewis's voice held a note of relief. "So, then do we have a motion regarding the position of zoo director for Cougar Bay Zoological Park?"

Mrs. Cowell smiled widely at Jason. "I move that we appoint Jason Andover as zoo director, effective immediately."

To Jason's surprise, Mr. Young said, "I'll second that."

Lewis asked, "All in favor please indicate by a show of hands."

Every person around the table raised a hand.

Lewis instructed his assistant, "Let the record show the vote was unanimous." He nodded across the table to Jason. "Congratulations."

As Jason shook the hand of the man next to him, a huge burden lifted. He thought of the sketched map of the African Lion Habitat in the top drawer of Lil's—now *his*—desk.

We're getting closer, Lil. We might just get it done. And I'm going to do everything in my power to help Kelli make it through these six months. Yes, they'd have a better start on their project financially if she didn't make it, but he refused to consider that.

Lewis left no time for pondering but plowed forward. "Now, the next order of business is an update on the AZA application process. Jason, do you want to bring us up to date on the status?"

Jason pulled the paperclip off the stack of papers in front of him and forced his mind to focus on the task at hand.

Chapter Eleven

Cameron was a tall young man with an eager grin and an easy manner that made Kelli like him immediately. With a start, she realized he was probably only a few years younger than she was. His nonstop talk and enthusiastic approach to his job made him appear much younger as he took her on a tour to introduce her to the primates.

"These are the tamarins." He stopped in front of an enclosure with a half dozen squirrel-sized monkeys.

Kelli inspected the full ruffs of orange fur surrounding their faces. "They look sort of like lions."

Cameron grinned and tapped a sign on the wall beside the enclosure. "They're called golden lion tamarins."

"Hey, what's wrong with that one?" Kelli pointed toward one poor creature with patchy white skin showing through gaps in the fur on his back. "Does he have mange or something?"

"No, actually, he's a pretty new father. Their babies cling to their backs, and his kids were a little rough on him. They pulled his hair out. Look, there are the babies."

Kelli had not noticed a pair of smaller tamarins about half the size of the adults high on a ledge. "Aw, how cute."

"Yeah. We're getting a little overpopulated, though." Cameron shrugged. "A pair is being transferred to a zoo up in the Florida panhandle."

Cameron fell quiet, his stare into the exhibit wistful. He must be attached to the little things, much the same as Raul. Kelli couldn't imagine what Raul would say if a pair of his precious charges was transferred to another zoo.

They moved down the path to join a line of zoo goers standing at a waist-high wall. A wide moat separated the wall from a grassy area with tall trees and a big wooden platform that looked like a treehouse. Seated on the platform was a creature that looked, at first glance, like a ginormous version of the tamarins Kelli had just seen. A second glance showed her this animal was nothing like the cute little tamarins. A large head, prominent mouth, long arms, all of it covered in reddish-brown hair. The creature looked just like Clyde, a character in a series of Clint Eastwood movies she enjoyed.

"It's an orangutan."

Cameron nodded. "That's Cocoa."

Kelli's interest pricked to attention. Cocoa was the name her mother had mentioned in her letter. She studied the animal carefully. "Tell me about her."

"Cocoa is eleven years old. She came to Cougar Bay about five years ago, back when they built this habitat. She weighs about a hundred and ten pounds and is strong as an ox. Orangutans are from the rain forests in Asia."

Kelli listened as Cameron lapsed into an encyclopedic description of the habitat and capabilities of orangutans in the wild. After a moment, her mind wandered. What could Lillian possibly have wanted her to learn from this ape?

She'd thought Cocoa was sleeping, but suddenly the orangutan swung over the side of the platform, suspended by her long, hairy arms. The crowd *oohed* as Cocoa hurdled sideways, grabbed on to the thick branch of one of the trees and pulled herself upward. She didn't stop there, but climbed up the trunk, her powerful legs working as hard as her hands. The people surrounding Kelli and Cameron laughed as she gave a giant leap and ended up back in her original position on the platform.

Kelli spoke without taking her eyes off the ape. "She's putting on a show."

"She sure is." Cameron laughed. "Cocoa's a big ham. Loves having an audience."

Cocoa settled on her side, back toward the crowd, and became still. Apparently she was through performing for the moment. After a few minutes, the people standing nearby wandered off toward the next exhibit.

Kelli leaned over the concrete wall and looked down. "That's a big area just for her."

Cameron shook his head. "This is nothing. Wild orangutans have large territories, about five square miles. They're solitary animals and like their space."

Kelli studied Cocoa, who seemed content to snooze in the shade. Was that what her mother was trying to tell her? That she needed her own space?

If she wanted to live her life alone, then she shouldn't have had a child.

As she watched, Cocoa lifted an arm, scratched her side, and dropped it back to the platform. Kelli decided she preferred the little tamarins. At least they shared their territories and took care of their children, even if it meant sacrificing a bit of hair.

Early Tuesday morning, Kelli punched in the code to let her through the zoo's employee entrance. She looked toward her mother's battered old Toyota parked between Jason's car and an older-model pickup. Seemed a ridiculous waste of gasoline to drive around to the front of the property when the zoo was practically in her backyard. She made a mental note to ask Jason about a key.

A peacock cry from somewhere in the distance carried to her on the damp morning air as she made her way to the office.

It wasn't yet seven-thirty, so she wasn't surprised to see Angela's desk empty. The door to the director's office stood open, though, and she heard the soft thud of a drawer sliding shut. Jason was already there. Hopefully he wouldn't mind if she worked with Raul again today. Maybe he'd even let her stay in the Small Animal building all day.

She stepped into the doorway and caught sight of Jason sitting behind the desk which, she noticed, no longer looked like wild animals had been turned loose to wreak havoc in a paper factory. It must have taken him hours to clean it off, but everything looked neat and orderly. Apparently, tidiness was one trait Jason shared with her and not her mother. The thought made her smile.

He became aware of her presence and looked up from his study of the single sheet of typewritten paper in the center of his desk. Bloodshot eyes brightened when he caught sight of her, and his expression changed from polite inquiry to genuine welcome that sent a shaft of warmth through her core.

"Kelli! What are you doing here?"

She lifted a shoulder. "I've always been an early bird. I've been up since five." She peered more closely at him. Darkened skin seemed to sag beneath his eyes. "No offense, but you look like you haven't slept at all."

He raked his fingers through hair that wasn't as orderly as usual, and confessed, "I haven't. Yesterday afternoon, the board of directors made my promotion official." His smile turned sheepish. "I guess I was too excited to sleep. I've been here since about three."

So, it was official. Lillian's plan was progressing. Kelli was surprised to discover the thought didn't anger her, as it would have a few days before. In fact, she found something about his confession appealing. He was like a little boy, too excited to sleep at Christmas.

"Congratulations," she said with as much warmth as she could convey, then went on with a touch of teasing. "Looks like my mother chose her successor well. You're as much a workaholic as she was." She took the two steps into the room to drop into the chair in front of his desk.

Amusement danced in his eyes, but otherwise his expression didn't change. He rocked back in his chair and folded his hands across his flat stomach. "And you're not? Your lights are staying on pretty late at night."

Heat threatened to flood Kelli's face. Should she be flattered that he noticed or insulted that he was comparing her to her workaholic mother? "And why were you looking at my house at night?"

Startled, his gaze dropped to the surface of the desk between them. "I, uh, was making my rounds. The light's visible in the dark from the kangaroo yard."

She, too, looked away. At the thought of him standing in the dark, looking up at her windows, a tickle erupted in her stomach. The sensation wasn't entirely unpleasant. Time to switch to a safer topic. "So, I was thinking I could go help Raul again this morning. He sort of asked if I would."

"Really?" She risked a glance up to find Jason regarding her with surprise. "I'm shocked. I figured he'd be in here first thing, demanding that I assign you somewhere else. How did you manage to get on Mr. Crusty's good side?"

She allowed a small smile. "He's not so bad." With a finger, she smoothed the crease in her tan slacks and avoided his amused gaze.

"Well, I'm sorry, but he can't have you today. I've got a special project I need your help with."

Interested, she looked up. A special project, working with Jason? One that didn't involve making worm salads or hearing a lecture on the animals' messier habits, maybe? "What is it?"

"We need to transport a pair of tamarins to another zoo today, and our procedures state that two zoo employees must be on hand for the transfer."

"But surely Cameron—"

His shaking head cut her off. "We're short-handed. I can't spare him today." His lips twisted into a rueful grimace. "Since you and I are the only ones in the animal care department without any animals depending on us, I'm afraid it's up to us." He placed his hands on the edge of his desk and scooted the chair backward. "It'll take a couple of hours to drive up there, and maybe a couple of hours on-site. We'll be back by mid-afternoon."

Six hours with Jason and nothing but a pair of squirrel-sized monkeys to run interference between them. Funny, but given the choice, she almost preferred spending the day in Raul's surly presence. At least he didn't watch her with a too-personal stare that made her insides quiver and her palms go moist.

"But Raul is expecting me."

A grin twitched at the corners of his lips, but it didn't break through. Without looking away from her face, he picked up the radio on the edge of his desk, pressed the talk button and informed Raul that his trainee would be assigned elsewhere today.

After a moment, Raul's gruff voice barked from the speaker, "Fine."

Jason set the radio back down. "There. Now, I've got one or two things to take care of here. I'll meet you at the primate area at eight."

Kelli swallowed her discomfort. *Remember, this is just for six months. Then life can return to normal.*

She stood and started to leave when the radio squawked and a female voice asked something about thawed meat for the wolves. Another voice answered.

Kelli nodded toward the radio. "So, when do I get one of those, like everyone else?"

"Not for a while. Trainees don't get radios, or keys either. You won't need them, because you won't be taking care of any animals on your own for a while." As he spoke, he swiveled his chair around to the file cabinet, the paper from the desk in hand.

In other words, he doesn't trust me.

Disgruntled at the brusque dismissal, or maybe at the reminder that she was nothing more than a lowly trainee, Kelli left the room repeating to herself, *Six months. It's just for six months.*

"Kelli, you want to grab that end?"

The pair of tamarins had been shifted into a smaller cage for transport with a lot of coaxing from Cameron. They hadn't wanted any part of the strange metal contraption, even if there were bananas and apples inside. In the end, Cameron had been forced to enter their enclosure and herd the chosen pair, while the others screeched at him from above and threw pieces of vegetables from their breakfast into his hair. Kelli, watching from a safe distance, couldn't hold back her laughter at their antics.

But finally the two had been separated, coaxed into the cage and were ready to go to their new home. Jason stood at one end of the cage and nodded for her to pick up the other end.

Cameron leaped forward. "I can get it."

"No, that's okay. I got it." Kelli elbowed him out of the way and bent at the knees to grab the edge. Manual labor might not be her forte, but she wasn't about to let someone else do her job for her.

"On three, then."

Jason counted and they lifted the cage in unison. It was heavier than Kelli expected and she let out an "Umph!" as she straightened.

Jason walked backward toward a white van with the zoo's logo on the side. The rear doors stood open, and when they arrived, he set his end on the edge and then came around to stand beside her and help slide it inside.

As he did, his arm pressed against hers. A jolt shot through Kelli at the contact of his warm skin. Startled, she almost let go, but managed to keep her grip on her corner of the cage. As soon as the container was safely inside the vehicle, she stepped away, out of reach, and stood watching, absently rubbing her arm.

Cameron, who had trailed them to the van, hopped inside and secured the cage with straps to keep it from sliding around during the drive.

"It's okay, you two." His low voice held a note of tenderness as he crooned to the pair huddled tightly together in the far corner, shivering. "Your new home's going to be great and you'll have the whole place to yourself. No more sharing."

He almost sounded as though he was trying to convince himself. Kelli risked a glance at his face and intercepted a struggle going on there. The poor kid looked like he was trying not to cry.

When he jumped down out of the van, Jason awarded him a sympathetic clap on the arm. "It's true, you know. They'll be fine."

Cameron's throat moved. He nodded but didn't reply. With a final long look inside the van, he shut the doors.

"You ready to go?" Jason asked her.

Kelli nodded. She climbed into the passenger seat and busied herself with adjusting her seat belt and arranging the air-conditioner vents as Jason navigated over the zoo paths and onto the road.

As the miles stacked up behind them, Kelli's awkwardness slipped away. Jason apparently didn't feel the need to fill the silence between them with small talk, which was fine with her. She considered asking him to turn on the radio, but then figured it might bother the tamarins, so her request went unspoken. A glance into the back showed her that they were starting to investigate their surroundings.

"They're moving around," she told Jason.

He kept his eyes on the road as he answered. "Good. They're young and inquisitive. They'll adjust to their new home in no time."

"Cameron looked really upset. I thought he might cry."

He tilted his head like a shrug but didn't reply.

"You don't seem very upset, though." She watched his profile as she made the comment. "I figured you'd be attached to all the animals at Cougar Bay."

"Oh, I am. But this is a good move for those two. They'll be this zoo's first tamarins, with a brand-new exhibit. They're going to be popular and get a lot of attention and excellent care. AZA has approved them as a breeding pair." He paused, then confessed, "There are some animals in our collection that I'd have a real problem transferring. I probably wouldn't be able to hold it together as well as Cameron did."

Kelli ran through the list of animals she'd encountered so far. "Is Cocoa one of them?"

Creases in his forehead cleared as though he hadn't considered that happening. "Well, yeah. I guess she is."

From his tone, Kelli had the impression Cocoa wasn't who he had in mind, but because the subject had come up, maybe she could get more out of him than she'd managed to gain from her conversation with Cameron.

She twisted in her seat as far as the seat belt would allow, her back resting against the door so she could look at him face-on. "Tell me about Cocoa. What's her story?"

He settled back in the driver's seat, his hands loose on the steering wheel. "Her habitat was the first major addition Cougar Bay made after Lil became the director. They had to tear down several exhibits and relocate some animals to do it, and for a while the public wasn't happy about it. But Lil proved right in the end." He flashed a smile in her direction. "Cocoa quickly became a favorite. She's got personality plus."

Kelli remembered her antics the day before. "I saw that. But I can understand why the public would be hesitant. That's a lot of space to take up for one animal."

"Well, she wasn't supposed to be just one animal. She was supposed to have a mate."

"Really?" Kelli tried to remember exactly what Cameron had told her. "I thought wild orangutans were solitary, that they didn't share their space."

"Males are, but a mother and her offspring will live together for up to seven years in the wild. And in captivity, they don't have to forage for food, so they adapt to living in close proximity to others. Most of them, anyway." He pressed the turn signal lever, glanced into the side mirror and changed lanes as he went on. "Cocoa was pregnant when we first got her."

Kelli's ears perked up. Maybe this was the story Lillian wanted her to hear. "What happened? Did she lose the baby?"

"No, the baby was born healthy. But Cocoa rejected him. In fact, she shoved him around her enclosure like she didn't know what he was and didn't much care. When he tried to cling on to her, like baby orangs do, she knocked him off. She was so rough the staff was afraid she'd kill him, and she probably would have. Plus, she wouldn't feed him. They had to take him away from her." His lips softened. "That was before I came to work at Cougar Bay, but I wish I'd been there. The entire staff underwent training to hand-raise that baby. They learned how mother orangs handle their babies, and wore a fur vest when they were on baby duty so he could hang on just like in the wild. And they bottle-fed him. Apparently, it was quite an experience."

So, Cocoa, her mother's first big project, had rejected her own baby. Kelli's lips tightened into a hard line. Was that the message Lillian was sending to Kelli, that it happened in the wild, so that somehow justified her actions?

Sorry, Mother, but I am not an ape!

If Lillian expected Kelli to insert herself into this story, she had been sadly mistaken. Humans were rational beings, not animals. They had responsibilities, and those who didn't live up to them deserved contempt, as far as Kelli was concerned.

Still, she couldn't stop herself from asking, "What happened to him? The baby."

Jason expelled a deep sigh. "While they were caring for him, they tried to work with Cocoa. They gave her a doll and taught her how to treat it. They hoped to get her to accept him as a younger cage mate that needed care, if not as her own baby." He shook his head. "It didn't work. And about that time a baby orang at a zoo in New Mexico died, so they shipped the baby out there to see if the mother, who'd given birth successfully twice before, would accept him." He nodded in satisfaction. "She did."

Just like Lillian had shipped Kelli off to live with Nana.

"That's a terrible story."

Her voice came out fiercer than she intended. Jason looked at her in surprise, and to hide her embarrassment, she twisted around in her seat and faced the front.

"It happens every now and then." He lifted a shoulder. "Some animals just aren't cut out to be mothers. Cocoa was born in captivity herself, so who knows? Maybe she missed something in her upbringing, something she would have received in the wild. She's still a great orangutan. One day soon, we hope to try introducing another orang into the exhibit, an older one. In the meantime, she's happy and healthy and loves performing for the crowds. The people are crazy about her."

Kelli tilted her nose in the air. "Well, I'm not."

He laughed out loud. "Apparently not. You look like you want to take her apart piece by piece." She was aware of him studying her profile. "Oh, I see. You've been through something like that yourself." When he spoke again, his voice was soft. "Kelli, you can't compare your mother to an animal."

Her head snapped sideways. "I certainly can. She told me in that letter to ask someone about Cocoa and then maybe I'd understand why she dumped her kid off for someone else to raise. Her kid who'd been traumatized and needed her desperately." The last word choked off in a sob. Horrified, Kelli felt tears prickle in her eyes and blinked them back with fury. She *would not* cry in front of Jason!

Silence fell between them. The sound of the tires on the road filled the van, punctuated by a metallic rattle in the cargo area, and the occasional shuffle of the tamarins as they moved around the cage. Kelli wrestled her emotions and finally got herself under an iron control she'd mastered long ago. There was no place in her life for tears over the past. They'd all been shed years before.

When Jason broke the silence, his voice was soft as a caress.

"I really wish I'd been around back then. I would have loved to take care of that baby."

The steel bands around her heart relaxed their hold. The warmth that flooded her face this time had nothing to do with embarrassment.

Chapter Twelve

The Wildlife Park Zoo was small even by Cougar Bay's standards. But Jason noted the neatly trimmed flowering shrubs lining the walkway that led to the ticket booth, the fresh-looking paint on the attractive iron fencing, the small but clean covered welcome area on the other side of the entrance turnstile. Curbside appeal was everything, and the zoo-going public in this area apparently approved. The parking lot was over half-full, and several adults with children in tow stood in line to buy tickets.

Jason drove around to an unobtrusive side entrance as he'd been instructed, backed up the van to the gate and reached for his cell phone to let his contact know they'd arrived. He needn't have bothered. The gate swung open before he could even punch in the phone number. A man in a beige T-shirt with the zoo's insignia greeted him and Kelli by the van's rear door.

"Jason Andover, right?" He thrust out a hand. "Tony Simpson. We're sure glad to see you."

He jerked his head toward a cluster of identically dressed people watching from a short distance away, their expressions eager.

Jason grinned. Obviously, the tamarins' arrival was anticipated. Cameron would be pleased to know his babies were receiving an enthusiastic welcome.

"This is Kelli Jackson," he told the man and opened the back door as the two shook hands.

"Oh, look at them!" Tony didn't bother to hide his glee as he gazed at the tamarins, who had retreated to the far corner of their cage, their arms wrapped around each other for support. "They're such beauties. Hey, a couple of you guys come give us a hand."

The last was directed toward the onlookers, and all four eagerly rushed forward. Jason caught Kelli's eye to exchange a grin as they all *oohed* over the new arrivals.

Tony hopped up in the van and unstrapped the ties holding the cage in place while one of the staff dashed back inside the gate and returned with a rolling cart, like a small flatbed on wheels. Jason and Kelli stood aside as they loaded the cage onto it, then Jason grabbed the folder containing the paperwork from the van. They both fell in step with Tony as the small group proceeded through the zoo over a neatly maintained path. People turned to watch the parade, and a couple of children exclaimed over the monkeys, but Jason noted with approval that two of the staff members stationed themselves on either side of the cage and firmly but politely kept anyone from disturbing the tamarins.

Tony spoke to Kelli. "So, have these two been in your care over at Cougar Bay? My folks have some questions they'd like to ask you."

Kelli shook her head. "No, sorry. I'm just along for the ride."

Tony's eyebrows rose, and Jason explained. "We're short-handed just now, so our primate keeper couldn't get away. But I'll answer whatever questions you have, and he'll be happy to talk to your people on the phone to fill in any details I can't."

The man's expression became contrite. "I guess Ms. Mitchell's death has left a big hole over there." He gulped. "I know you'll miss her. She was well thought of. A fine animal advocate."

Jason opened his mouth to inform Tony who Kelli was, but she caught his eye and gave a nearly imperceptible shake of her head.

Now, why doesn't she want him to know Lil was her mother?

Jason understood almost nothing about the relationship between his former boss and her daughter, but after their conversation in the van he was beginning to see just how deep Kelli's wounds went. When she'd been sitting ramrod straight in the seat beside him with pain etched on her face, he'd had the oddest urge to pull over to the side of the road and wrap his arms around her. He knew instinctively that she would reject that kind of comfort from him. The least he could do was comply with her wishes and keep his mouth shut.

To Tony, he simply agreed. "Yes, she was."

The new tamarin exhibit was even bigger than the one at Cougar Bay, Jason noted with approval. The indoor area, with thick safety glass for zoo visitors to look through, held a variety of cage furniture. Trees, poles, a vine, artificial rock outcroppings, along with enough space for at least a dozen tamarins to swing and scamper. Jason also noted a panel, shut at the moment, leading to an outdoor yard.

A small crowd had followed them, and one of the zoo employees instructed everyone to please stand back while they introduced the tamarins to their new home. Jason joined Kelli at one side of the glass and stood close to her as they watched the staff lift the cage from the cart, through the access area, and place it on the floor inside the exhibit. Tony waited until everyone else had left. As he knelt in front of the cage to unlatch the door, Jason saw his lips moving as he spoke in calm tones to the pair of frightened monkeys inside. As soon as the cage was opened, he stepped out of the exhibit and into the access area. A hush fell over the watching crowd as they waited for the tamarins to move.

This was a good opportunity to instruct Kelli on some of the procedures involved in transferring an animal. Jason kept his voice low. "When we receive a new animal, it's quarantined for thirty days before we introduce it into the exhibit. They probably have a similar procedure here, but since these are their first tamarins and there are no other species nearby—" he glanced at the nearest exhibit, which was at least fifty feet away "—there's no reason not to put them in their new home immediately."

Kelli gave a slight nod, her eyes fixed on the huddled pair in the cage. "They're not coming out." She sounded worried.

Jason smiled down at her. "They will."

Tony approached and gestured toward the folder Jason held. "Are the vet records in there? Our veterinarian will be here soon."

Jason tapped the folder against his palm. "Everything's right here. And I need your signature on a couple of forms."

Jason left Kelli with the Wildlife Park staff while he and Tony stepped into a small workroom to deal with the paperwork. When he returned, she had not moved.

She looked up at him, a wide smile lighting her features. "They like it!"

Jason's heart did a flip-flop at that smile, the first genuine one he'd seen her wear. He spared a glance at the tamarins, who had exited the metal cage and were in the process of climbing branches of the artificial smooth-sided tree, but he couldn't look away from Kelli for long. Delight transformed her face, and the sight made his breath catch in his chest.

At that moment, he would have gone into a cage and climbed a tree himself if he could just make her smile like that *at him*.

When the part-time veterinarian employed by Wildlife Park Zoo arrived, she gave the tamarins a quick inspection and assured everyone that the pair weren't suffering any ill effects from the trip. Jason and Kelli bade goodbye to Tony and the rest of the staff. They loaded the empty cage in the back of the van and took off. Because it was past lunchtime, Jason pulled into the first fast-food restaurant he saw and parked.

He glanced at her before turning off the engine. "I don't know about you, but I'm starving. This okay?"

Kelli looked through the windshield at the sign and shrugged. "Anything's fine with me."

The enchanting smile had disappeared from her face when they left the tamarin exhibit, and Jason found himself wanting to do something to bring it back. He leaned forward and held the glass door open for her to enter ahead of him. She passed by close enough for him to smell the clean, fresh scent that clung to her hair. It reminded him of spring breezes blowing through blooming lilac bushes.

Carrying the tray with their lunch piled on it, he followed Kelli to a table against the rear wall and slid into a molded plastic chair.

"I'm surprised you didn't want to stick around and scope out the zoo," she said as she unwrapped her burger. "I would have thought, being a zoo guy, you'd want to check out the competition."

"Oh, we're not in competition with each other. The way we look at it, what's good for one zoo is good for animals everywhere." He peeled the paper off his straw and shoved it in his cup. "Actually, I didn't want to let on in front of Tony or his staff, but I drove up there a few weeks ago to check out the place, back when we first got the notice of the transfer."

Her lips twitched sideways. "Why doesn't that surprise me?"

She peeled off the top bun and removed two pickles. With arched eyebrows, she extended them in his direction.

"Sure." He opened his burger and let her arrange the pickles on the melted cheese. She didn't just toss them on, he noted, but carefully placed them so they were evenly spaced with his other two. For some reason, that made him bite back a smile. She was certainly organized.

He searched for a safe topic of conversation, something that might draw out that smile again.

"Tell me about your grandmother."

Her head tilted sideways as she considered. A wave of dark hair dangled in her face, and she tucked it behind her ear with an absent gesture. "Nana's almost eighty-two years old, but don't let that fool you. She refuses to act her age and she stays busy all the time. Quilting, knitting, cooking. She's always got some project going on."

"Since she didn't come to Lil's memorial service, I assume she's your father's mother."

"That's right."

The clipped words and closed expression as she bit into her sandwich stopped him from asking any of the other questions that pressed on him, like who her father was and if he was still living. She obviously didn't want to discuss him.

He picked up a fry. "You know, I think our church has a group of women who quilt. I've seen it mentioned in the bulletin."

He shoved the fry into his mouth. What was he doing? Just two days ago he'd decided to discourage her from attending his church.

She nodded as she chewed and swallowed. "I saw it Sunday. It'll be good for her to get involved. She needs to meet people, since I'll be working so much. And the church is close enough to the house that maybe someone would be willing to give her a ride." Her eyes rolled upward. "She's stubborn enough to want to drive herself, but she doesn't see as well as she used to. I definitely don't want her behind the wheel in the traffic down here."

Well, okay. If her grandmother needed something to keep her busy, where was the harm? Besides, he was having trouble remembering why he'd decided in the first place that Kelli shouldn't go to his church. "We have a lot of older people in our congregation, so I'm sure there are rides available. This *is* Florida, you know, the retirement capital of the world."

To prove his point, he slid his eyes around the room, where at least half of the other diners were elderly. Kelli followed his gaze and nodded, his point taken.

"I'm sure she'll make friends in no time," Jason told her. "Are you driving back, so you can bring some furniture with you?"

"For six months?" Kelli shook her head. "We'll make do with what my mother had. Nana will take the bedroom. I found a furniture rental place in the phone book, so I'll probably just get a twin bed or something after I get back. Until then—" She shrugged. "The sofa's pretty comfortable."

They ate in silence for a moment.

"Your mother seems nice," Kelli said.

"Thanks. She said the same about you."

Kelli kept her eyes down, staring at her sandwich. "Do you mind if I ask you a question?"

"Go ahead."

"Did she lose someone recently?"

Jason set down his cup. How in the world did she know that? "Yes, actually, we both did. My dad died right before Christmas, after a long illness."

She dragged a French fry through a mound of ketchup on the spread-out sandwich wrapper. "I thought so. She looked like someone who was familiar with grief." She glanced up. "I'm sorry about your father."

"Thanks."

For a moment, he considered pointing out that they'd both lost a parent recently, that they shared that in common. But given the estranged relationship between Kelli and Lil, their situations didn't seem all that similar.

"At least you have your mother. And she has you." The fry was thoroughly covered with ketchup now, but she made no move to lift it to her lips, just kept dragging it back and forth, spreading out the thick red puddle. "It's important to have the support of those you love."

A shadow passed over her features, leaving behind such a deep sadness that Jason wanted to reach across the table and wipe it away. *Oh, Kelli, what happened between you and Lil to hurt you so deeply?*

In the next instant, her face cleared and she looked up with a determined smile that held none of the warmth of the one he'd witnessed earlier. "Change of subject. Since your mom is involved in a matchmaking group, how is it you've escaped unscathed?"

Since her sadness faded as she introduced a new topic, Jason welcomed her question. His lunch finished, he wadded up his burger wrapper, shoved it in the fry container and pushed the trash to one side. "Who says I'm unscathed?" He assumed a mock-serious frown. "Trust me, I've been caught in their snares a time or two and I have the scars to prove it."

She laughed. "You don't expect me to believe that the man who handles wild animals on a daily basis has been wounded by a pack of wily women?"

"It's true. I narrowly escaped with my bachelorhood intact."

She folded her arms on the table and leaned forward to catch his gaze with her clear one. "Seriously. You're probably a few years older than me, which means you're close to thirty. I'll bet most of your friends are married by now. Why not you? And don't tell me you haven't found the right woman." Her eyes narrowed. "If I'm right, not only are you not looking, you probably run in the other direction whenever a woman bats her eyelashes at you."

Memories flooded his mind, of Aimee's fluttering eyelashes. He broke away from Kelli's gaze and stared at the trio of teenagers seated at the table behind her. "You're right. But trust me, I wasn't always a workaholic. Not too many years ago I dated quite a bit."

She leaned back and gave a nod. "I thought so. What happened? No, let me guess." Her voice took on a trace of bitterness. "You took a job with my mother at Cougar Bay, and she turned you into a workaholic."

"I can't blame that on Lil." He dropped his head forward to stare at the table. "I used to be pretty wild. Made some major mistakes and hurt someone who didn't deserve it." He shook his head. "She's never forgiven me."

After a moment of silence, Kelli's hand snaked across the table to cover his. "I'm sorry. I shouldn't have pried."

The skin of her palm was soft on the back of his hand, her touch featherlight. Jason almost turned his hand over to entwine those slender fingers in his, but before he could react, she jerked away. She leaned back and dropped both hands into her lap.

"It's okay," he said. "That whole mess is what made me finally give in to Mom's begging and start going to church. I became a believer because of it."

"Have you explained that to—her?" Kelli paused. "The girl?"

Jason thought of the time when he'd sat down with Aimee to share his newfound faith. His attempts were met with the same derision as his previous apologies. She'd thrown his words back in his face and let him know in no uncertain terms that she wanted to have as little to do with him as possible, and she wished with all her heart that she never had to see him again.

To Kelli, he said, "Oh, yeah." Then he reached for her trash and piled it on the plastic tray. "My turn to change the subject. When you get back from Denver, I'll have your schedule laid out for you."

They stood, and Kelli fell in beside him as he headed for the trash can to dump their garbage.

"Won't I be working with Raul?" She sounded hopeful, at which he hid a smile. At least she'd gotten over the disdain he'd seen that first morning.

"Some," he promised as they exited the restaurant. "But I want you to go through the same training program as any other keeper, which means you'll learn to care for every animal in the collection. That way if we have an unexpected absence, like the other day when Raul was hurt, you'll be able to pitch in and help."

He had almost reached the van when he realized she was no longer at his side. He turned to find her standing on the sidewalk, staring at him with wide eyes.

"All of the animals?" Her voice squeaked on the last word.

"That's right."

"Even the—" her gulp was obvious "—lion?"

He cocked his head to stare at her. She'd gone pale.

"Of course. And the cougars and the other cats. But don't worry, Samson is—"

He didn't get to finish his sentence. Kelli wavered as though she would pass out, and he rushed forward to support her. She leaned heavily against his arm, and he felt her body tremble as she clung to him.

"Kelli, what is it? Are you sick?"

She turned, his arm still around her, and placed both hands on his shoulders. Her fingers bit into his flesh as her eyes pierced his.

"I won't work with the lion." Each word was punctuated by a shake. "Do you understand? No amount of money can make me do it. Promise me right now, Jason, or I won't come back from Denver."

Naked fear lashed at him from her eyes. No, this went deeper than fear. She was shaking violently, clearly panic-stricken at the idea of working with a lion.

What happened to her?

Undoubtedly, this was the fear Lil wanted her to face. But looking down into Kelli's terror-stricken expression, he knew he couldn't force her to do it against her will. Did Lil have any idea how deep Kelli's fear went? What kind of mother would ask him to torture her child like that?

He held her gaze. "I promise, Kelli. If you don't want to work with the lion, I won't make you."

Sorry, Lil. I know you trusted me, but it's wrong. I can't do that to her.

He pulled her forward and wrapped both arms around her shivering body. She didn't resist, but buried her face in his shoulder.

Chapter Thirteen

Kelli spent the afternoon in the commissary, elbow-deep in rotting fruit. They'd arrived back at Cougar Bay in time to help unload a truckload of fresh fruits and vegetables, donated from a local grocery store. The outdated produce had been removed from the store's shelves, and somebody needed to separate the truly inedible from the bruised or partially rotten.

"Everybody else has animals to take care of." Jason had told her with an apologetic grimace. "We're short-handed, you know."

Kelli had heaved a sigh loud enough to make her point. "So I've heard."

After sorting through more rotten strawberries and oozing tomatoes than she could count, she finally finished. The edible berries piled in a plastic bin went into the walk-in cooler. She slid it onto a chilly metal shelf beside a pile of kale leaves and exited the cooler to find Jason waiting for her beside the work table.

"You got it done," he said, glancing at the empty wooden surface.

She screwed up her face into a scowl. "I may never eat fruit again after some of the stuff I've handled today. And the smell." She made a show of gagging.

One of Jason's eyebrows rose. "Worse than the Small Animal building?"

She conceded his point with a tilt of her head. "Okay, maybe there are worse smells than rotten potatoes."

Sticky strawberry juice had stained her fingers pink and stood in puddles on the worktable. She went to the sink and ran hot water over a ragged dishcloth. When she turned back toward the table, Jason was leaning against it, arms folded across his chest, his expression thoughtful. Her heart launched into an imitation of African bongo drums. What thoughts were going through that oh-so-handsome head of his? Was he remembering her breakdown at lunch?

Embarrassment at her outburst washed over her and she busied herself with wiping off the table. So much for all those expensive therapy sessions. She still fell apart at the idea of going near a lion.

Or was she more embarrassed by the way she'd clung to Jason, nestled within the safety of his arms?

He broke into her thoughts with a welcome interruption. "What time is your flight tomorrow?"

"Nine-twenty."

"So you'll need to be at the airport by eight. You should leave around seven-fifteen."

The worktable was clean. She nodded as she shook the cloth out over the trash can. "Even earlier, I figure, because of the traffic."

He bent over to pick up a piece of cellophane that had fallen on the floor. "I was wondering if you need a ride."

Startled, her grip loosened and she dropped the rag into the can on top of a pile of fragrant rotten fruit. A nice offer, and it would save her the cost of the taxi she'd already reserved. It was a forty-minute ride from here to the airport, so the fare would be expensive. Forty minutes of silence with a cab-driving stranger.

Or forty minutes with Jason.

Her pulse fluttered at the thought. She turned away slightly so he wouldn't see the conflict raging on her face.

He's my mother's handpicked replacement, she reminded herself. *He's after the money, that's all. He wants me to fail.*

But she no longer believed that, not really. When had she changed her mind about Jason? Maybe this afternoon, when he'd held her close and told her she didn't have to work with the lion if she didn't want to. She closed her eyes, remembering the feel of his arms around her.

He's a zookeeper. I can't ever forget that. I could never love a zoo-keeper. Not after Lillian. And Daddy.

Her resolve strengthened, she flashed a smile in his direction as she retrieved her cloth from the trash can. "Thanks anyway, but I've already arranged for a ride. I appreciate the offer, though."

He studied her for a moment before giving a slow nod. "All right, if you're sure."

"Uh-huh." She went back to the sink, relieved for the excuse to turn her back on him while she rinsed the cloth.

"Well, have a good trip, then. I guess I'll see you in a week."

Kelli started to let him leave. Then she remembered something. She whirled around. "Wait."

He stopped in the doorway, his expression suddenly eager. "Change your mind?"

"No." She crossed to the shelf where she'd stashed her purse, dug inside it and turned, holding up the key she'd put there this morning. "You'll need this back if you're going to feed the cat while I'm gone."

For an instant, his face fell. But then his good-natured smile returned and he held out a palm. When she placed the key in it, he closed warm fingers around hers and held them briefly, his eyes locked onto hers. Kelli thought surely he could hear her heart pounding against her ribs.

"Don't worry. I'll take care of everything." He squeezed her hand and then was gone.

The craziest thought entered Kelli's mind. Did Jason mean more than just feeding the cat?

"Anybody in here?"

A male voice, followed by the sound of the door shutting, jerked Jason out of the world of zoo procedures. He looked up from the computer monitor toward the open doorway, then glanced at his watch. Nine-thirty already? Where had the evening gone?

"Yeah, I'm here," he called.

Vic, the nighttime security guard, stepped into view. "You're making a habit of working late."

Jason leaned back in the chair and rubbed his tired eyes. "I got involved in section three of our accreditation application. But I'm about to call it a night. My eyes are going to cross if I stare at that screen another five minutes."

Vic's gaze swept the room, apparently noting the orderly appearance. He gave an approving nod. "Heard about your promotion. Congratulations."

"Thanks."

"You planning to walk the property tonight before you leave?"

"Yes. As usual."

"Well, you might want to take a look at the bench in front of the macaw cage. Some smart-aleck kid got creative with a magic marker or something. Needs to be painted."

Great. Another repair job to add to the list. "All right, I'll do that. Thanks for letting me know."

Vic left while Jason jotted down a reminder to ask maintenance if the bench could be cleaned or would need to be repainted. The outer door slammed shut, plunging the office into a deep silence. For a moment, Jason considered finishing the section he'd been working on, but then dismissed the idea. He needed to get home or Angela would come in tomorrow morning and find him sleeping at his desk. With no sleep at all last night and a long day today, he was exhausted.

A long day, but a good one. He and Kelli had turned a corner today. For the first time since she arrived, she'd given him a peek inside that tough shell she hid behind. Even before her panic attack, or whatever it had been. That gorgeous smile of hers while she watched the tamarins, and then the way she'd talked to him over lunch.

With a start, he realized he'd like to spend more time with her, and not just at work either. The realization brought a slow smile to his face. Who would have guessed he'd end up having feelings for Lil's daughter?

Would she even consider going out with him? He rolled the pen between his fingers as he pondered the question. A few days ago he would have answered no, no way. But after today, maybe. He may have been unable to tease a smile out of her, but he felt as though she'd started to trust him, maybe even like him. Why else would she cling to him outside the restaurant like that? And she'd felt so good in his arms, like she belonged there.

Of course, she turned down his offer for a ride tomorrow. He rocked backward in the desk chair, frowning.

Well, no reason to rush. Maybe when she returned from Denver he would invite her out for dinner to officially welcome her to Florida. He hadn't been on a date since...

Jason rocked forward and punched the keys to shut down the computer with savage force. Talking to Kelli about Aimee today had brought the whole mess back with a vividness that gnawed at his insides. And he didn't even have an opportunity to tell her the whole story. He hadn't mentioned Tiffany.

He glanced at his cell phone resting on the corner of the desk. The last time he talked to Tiffany had been … when? He squeezed his eyes shut, trying to remember. Two weeks ago. Right before Lil died. Life had been crazy since then, but he should have called last week. What would Kelli think of a man who only talked to his daughter every two weeks? Guilt washed over him. Probably not much.

He snatched up the phone and tapped the Contact icon to bring up Tiffany's number. Correction. Aimee's number. Setting his jaw, he punched the button to dial.

She picked up on the second ring.

"Hello?" Pleasant tone. She must be in a good mood.

"Hey, it's Jason."

A pause and then far less pleasantly, "Oh. Hello."

Jason clenched his teeth. "Can I talk to Tiffany?"

"At nine-forty?" Exasperation colored her tone. "You're kidding me, right? She's four years old. Bedtime was an hour ago."

Of course it was. I'm such an idiot. "Sorry. I lost track of time. So, uh, will you tell her in the morning that Daddy called, and I'll call her back tomorrow?"

"I'll tell her that *her father* called. Her daddy tucked her in tonight."

An unexpected jealousy surged like acid in Jason's stomach. "She calls Jeff Daddy?"

"Of course she does." Aimee clipped the words short, as though she wanted to spend as little time conversing with him as possible. Nothing new there. "He lives here. He reads her bedtime stories. He's her daddy in every way that matters."

And I'm just a stranger who used to know her mother. "I'm glad she has Jeff in her life. But I'm her father, Aimee. She needs to know who I am."

An exaggerated sigh blasted through the phone. "Why do you want to confuse her with labels? You're a nice man who comes to visit once a month and brings her presents. That's plenty for a four-year-old to grasp. Later, when she's older, we'll explain everything to her."

Jason propped an elbow on the chair arm and dropped his forehead into his hand. Tiffany lived two and a half hours away, on Florida's east coast. With his work schedule he couldn't get over there for visits more than once a month. Mom constantly urged him to insist on his visitation rights and bring her to stay with him for a weekend, but Aimee always said Tiffany was still too young. Was she? Would she cry for her mother? Her—daddy?

Jason massaged his temples with his fingers. He and Aimee never managed to have a pleasant conversation. There was too much history between them. Too much anger on her part; too much guilt on his.

"Just tell her I called," he said, too weary to argue. "I'll call her tomorrow."

The phone went dead when Aimee hung up without another word. Jason stared at the screen. If he wanted to have any sort of relationship with his daughter, he needed to get along with his ex-girlfriend. Correction. Aimee had never been his girl-friend. They'd met on the beach and had one shameful, drunken encounter that had ruined her life, according to her. How could he expect to have a relationship with Tiffany when her mother couldn't stand to look at him?

He swept the papers into the top drawer and dropped the pen on top. He should be glad Aimee had married last year. Jeff was a decent guy, a good stepfather for Tiffany. Maybe Jason should do as Aimee clearly wanted him to do, pay his child support but otherwise leave them alone to live a normal family life.

The drawer slammed shut with force, and he slammed his mind shut on that thought as well. No, Tiffany was his daughter. One day, when she was old enough, he'd explain everything without confusing her or upsetting her mother. Until then, he'd keep providing for her financially and visiting when he could.

He stood, dropped his phone into his pocket and headed for the door. No standing by the kangaroo yard to gaze at Kelli's windows tonight. He was so tired he couldn't even take his nightly walk through the zoo. All he could think about was getting home and falling into bed.

Chapter Fourteen

The taxi driver unloaded all their bags at the edge of the driveway, counted the money Kelli handed him and left without a word. She watched the yellow vehicle disappear down the street and fought the temptation to grumble. The least he could have done is haul the suitcases up the porch stairs for them.

"Well, isn't this a nice little house."

Nana stood beside her, staring at the house, every strand of her white hair firmly conformed into tight curls from the permanent she'd gotten yesterday before they left Denver. Her twinkling blue eyes betrayed none of the tiredness Kelli felt. Of course, Nana hadn't been up until midnight every night for the past week working on client accounts.

"It could use a bit of TLC, though," the elderly lady went on. "The paint is peeling terribly on those shutters."

"Looks like the weeds have been mowed." Kelli eyed the front yard, which at least didn't have the bare spots the backyard did. Although there didn't appear to be a single blade of real grass hiding among the weedy greenery. "I wonder if Jason did that."

Nana cast a quick glance her way, her lips tight with an unsuccessful attempt not to smile. "I can hardly wait to meet your young man. You've barely spoken a single sentence without mentioning him."

Blushing furiously, Kelli busied herself with slinging both their carry-on bags on her shoulders and pulling the biggest of the rolling suitcases up the walkway to the porch. Apparently she'd mentioned Jason once or twice in the past week, although she was certain it wasn't always in positive terms. She clearly remembered telling Nana of her early suspicions that he was some sort of gold digger, out for nothing but Lillian's money. But she'd also talked at some length about his nicer qualities, like his ready smile and caring manner. In fact, in the past few days, she'd found herself actually looking forward to her return to Florida so she could see him again.

She pulled the heavy suitcase up the single step to the small concrete porch. Even so, she must never forget that he was a zookeeper. A long-term relationship between them was completely out of the question.

But for the next six months—

"He's not my young man," she told Nana sternly. "He's my boss."

Nana simply smiled and extended the handle on one of the other rolling suitcases. Kelli chose to ignore her grandmother's smirk and unlocked the deadbolt.

"Here we are," she announced as she pushed the door open. "Home sweet home, at least for a little while."

She pulled the suitcase over the doorjamb and stepped into the living room, Nana right behind her. Everything was exactly as she'd left it, except—

"Oh, my! How beautiful." Nana spied the flowers on the kitchen counter at the same moment as Kelli. She left her suitcase where it was and hurried across the living room.

Kelli followed, warmth flooding through her that had nothing to do with the heat and humidity outside. She watched as Nana picked up a folded note propped in front of the vase of colorful blooms that looked like they'd come from a well-tended garden.

"It says, 'Welcome to Florida.' Well, isn't that sweet?" Nana handed the paper to her. "And look at this. My goodness, it appears your boss is trying to make an impression."

A deep smirk on her face, Nana pointed out a plate of oatmeal raisin cookies resting on the counter beside the flowers. They had the comfortingly irregular shape of homemade, not bakery. "I'm sure his mother made those. She's a nice lady," Kelli said absently as she studied the note. The handwriting was small, tight and masculine.

Nana said nothing, just turned a twinkling gaze on Kelli before she buried her nose in the blossoms.

"I'll get the other suitcases." Kelli hurried out to the driveway where the final two bags waited.

She wrestled them into the house and shut the door behind her. Nana appeared from the direction of the office.

"Your bedroom is over here," Kelli said, pulling Nana's suitcases toward the master bedroom. "I'm sorry to leave you the job of clearing out Mother's stuff. I meant to do it before I left, but I never had a chance."

"That won't be a problem," Nana assured her. "But I thought you said you were planning to sleep on the couch."

Kelli paused in the doorway to the bedroom. "I am, at least until I can get a bed of some sort for the office."

Creases deepened on Nana's brow. "Why do you want to sleep in the office instead of the beautiful daybed in the other bedroom?"

Kelli stared at her for a moment, uncomprehending. Then she left the suitcases where they were and hurried toward the cat's room. The sight stopped her in the doorway, where she stood, her jaw gaping.

The room had been transformed. A daybed with a white wooden frame occupied one corner, covered in a cheerful floral bedspread and fluffy throw pillows. A matching dresser, painted white with gold trim, rested on the wall beneath the back window, and against the opposite wall stood a charming dressing table with a stool and a tall mirror in a gilded frame.

"I don't understand," Kelli said, stunned. "This is the cat's room."

Nana squeezed past her and picked up a folded sheet of paper on the surface of the dressing table. She handed it to Kelli.

Kelli,

I don't care what you say, sofas are not comfortable. This furniture was gathering dust in my mother's garage. Now she can get her car in there. Use it for as long as you need it.

Jason

Nana stood beside her, peering sideways to read. "It's a nice young man who'd do that."

Numb, Kelli could only nod her agreement.

Chapter Fifteen

Twilight was just starting to darken the sky when a knock sounded on the back door.

Nana, who had claimed the wing chair and scooted it close to the tiny television screen, looked up. "Who could that be? It's after eight o'clock at night."

Kelli knew of only one person who would come to the back door at any time of the day or night. Her pulse quickened as she set her laptop on the sofa cushion beside her and hurried across the room. Stomach fluttering like a lovesick teenager's, she smoothed a hand over her unruly hair and wished for time to run a comb through it before opening the door.

Jason's presence in the doorway struck her like an unexpected gust of wind. The smile that curved his lips and lit his eyes deepened when he caught sight of her, sending a giddy tickle through her insides. For a moment all she could do was stare into his face. How could she have forgotten how handsome he was?

"Welcome back, Kelli." His southern drawl stretched out her name as though he wanted to relish the feel of it on his lips. "I hope you had a good trip."

"Thank you so much for everything." The words gushed out before she could temper them. "The flowers, the cookies and the *furniture!* I love it. Everything is just perfect." She snapped her mouth shut and gripped the door handle tighter as she also attempted to get a grip on her babbling tongue.

He put an arm against the door frame and leaned on it, a lopsided grin wreaking havoc on her insides. "I'm glad you like it."

Kelli pried her fingers off the doorknob and stepped back with a gesture. "Come on inside. I want you to meet my grandmother."

Nana had risen from her chair, and Jason approached her with an outstretched hand. "It's a pleasure to meet you, Mrs. Jackson. I'm Jason Andover."

Kelli closed the door and then turned to see Nana clasping his hand in both of hers while she inspected him with undisguised delight. Kelli closed her eyes and whispered a prayer that Nana wouldn't do anything to humiliate her, like mention how often Kelli had talked about him in the last week.

"Nice to meet you, too. And what a pleasant surprise we had waiting for us when we arrived this afternoon." She inclined her head toward the cookies that still lay on the counter, although the plate contained fewer treats than before. "The cookies were delicious and those flowers are just beautiful."

"My mom's the baker. She'll be happy to hear you enjoyed them." He lowered his voice and spoke in a charming conspiratorial tone. "Don't mention the flowers when you meet her, though. I swiped them from her yard."

Nana's laughter rang in the small room. "Your secret is safe with me."

"If you're not busy, I thought you ladies might like to join me for a walk around the zoo grounds." His gaze swept to Kelli to include her in his invitation. "This is the best time to see it, when the temperature starts to cool and the public has gone home."

"That's very kind of you, but I think I'll stay in tonight. The trip has tired me out." Nana gave Kelli a shrewd look that was impossible to mistake. "But I'm sure my granddaughter's legs could use some stretching. You two young people go ahead."

Kelli bit back an embarrassed groan at Nana's obvious ploy to throw them together. She made a lame attempt to protest with a gesture toward her laptop. "I've got work to do."

"Oh, come on. Take a break from all those boring numbers." Jason's words teased her even as he linked a hand through her arm and propelled her with gentle pressure toward the back door. "They'll be here when you get back."

"Well—" Kelli allowed herself to be guided, relishing the light pressure of his touch. "Maybe a short walk."

The sun hadn't set yet, but it hung low on the horizon, hidden from view behind the houses in Lillian's neighborhood. Jason led her through the back gate, across the access road and through the zoo's rear entrance. He didn't release her arm until he needed both hands to unlock the padlock, and after that, Kelli stepped out of reach. She needed to keep a clear head and her thoughts were muddled when she couldn't think of anything except the way her bare skin tingled beneath his touch.

He's a zookeeper. A zookeeper. She repeated the mantra as they set off down the path past the kangaroo yard. *A zookeeper and my boss.*

"I'm awfully glad you came back," Jason told her as they strolled past a small herd of curly-horned sheep.

Kelli glanced sideways at him. "Did you think I wouldn't?"

He cocked his head, but kept his gaze fixed on the trail ahead of them. "I thought you might get back around all those accountants in Denver and change your mind."

"You think I'm going to walk away from $700,000?"

He glanced her way. "You're not doing this for the money."

A thrill of pleasure shot through Kelli. His tone was so confident, so positive, like he'd spent a significant amount of time considering her reasons. At least he didn't think she was money-hungry. She couldn't bear it if Jason thought she was motivated only by money.

Even though I thought that of him. She almost winced at the thought.

"So, why am I doing it?" she asked.

His expression became distant as he considered his answer. "For Lil, a little. No matter what happened between you two, I think you want to honor her desire for you to understand why she loved this place so much." They walked a few more steps. "But mostly, I think you're doing it for yourself."

"What do you mean?" She tried not to bristle. Was he calling her self-centered? That was practically the same thing as money-hungry.

He stopped on the path and turned to face her. "You don't like disorder, not in your home or your office or, I'm guessing, anywhere in your life. I've watched you work. You're neat and thorough and you don't like to leave things unresolved."

Kelli might have been tempted to feel flattered, but she knew where this was leading and she wasn't sure she liked the direction. But Jason was right—she couldn't leave something unfinished any more than she could leave an account unbalanced.

"Go on," she told him, though with hesitation.

"Whatever it is that's unresolved between your mother and you, it's eating at you. It's not in your nature to turn your back on it and walk away. You want to face it head-on. Get past it. And you can't do that back in Denver." He spread his arms to indicate the zoo all around them. "You have to be here."

Kelli looked in the direction his hands swept. The tall, flowering hedge that lined the path cast sweet whiffs of scent on the gentle breeze that stirred the leaves. Ahead, a row of dome-shaped birdcages nestled in shaded alcoves. Beyond them, the three-sided enclosure that housed a pair of bears looked cave-like in the deep shadows of twilight.

"You're right," she finally admitted. "I do want to understand why my mother loved this place enough to choose it over her own daughter."

Jason's voice was soft. "I think there's more to it than that."

She gave him a sharp glance and turned forward to continue their walk. He was referring to her fear of lions, which she did not intend to discuss. "Maybe there is." Her tone didn't leave room for him to press her further.

They walked in silence for a few steps. "Someday I hope you'll trust me enough to tell me about it."

Kelli's step slowed. She'd never discussed the trauma that had destroyed her childhood with anyone except her counselor and Nana. Mostly, she preferred to stuff the memory into the recesses of her mind and pretend the incident had never happened. But the feelings hovered closer to the surface here at Cougar Bay, like an old, rusty car that had rested safely at the bottom of a lake for years and suddenly decided to float to the top and expose the secrets that had sent it there.

I need someone I can trust to be nearby when it surfaces.

Was Jason that someone? She thought of his arms around her, strong arms that sought to shelter her from the terrors of the past.

"Maybe someday I will," she whispered.

A waist-high wall around the bears' enclosure served as the first barrier between the animals and zoo guests. Kelli leaned against it and Jason stood beside her, close enough that she felt his breath like a caress on her cheek. The space between them vibrated with energy. The vivid memory of his embrace a week ago made it hard to listen to the warnings that sounded in her brain. But she ignored them as Jason peered deeply into her eyes. Her breath caught in her lungs as his lips drew hers closer, like the sandy shore draws an ocean wave.

In the moment before their lips touched, a sound split the air. The roar of a lion. A sickening jolt of fear shot through Kelli's stomach. She jerked backward and sucked in a breath.

"That was close. Where is he?"

The question quivered with fear. Had the lion gotten out of his enclosure? She glanced down the path behind Jason, but didn't glimpse tawny fur, thank goodness.

Jason drew back, eyes dark with regret. "His exhibit is just over there, beyond the cougars."

Kelli cast an anxious glance in that direction. She'd managed to avoid this part of the zoo so far, and hadn't realized they were this close.

"I think it's time to head home. It's getting dark." She made a show of looking up at the darkening sky, well aware that she wasn't fooling Jason at all. But at the moment, she didn't care. The sooner she put some distance between her and that lion, the better.

"Nighttime is my favorite time at the zoo," Jason told her, but he took her arm and led her back down the path, in the direction from which they'd come.

Kelli couldn't even force herself to enjoy the touch of his hand. It felt warm, but not warm enough to dispel the chill that had frozen her core at the sound of the lion's roar.

Jason walked Kelli through the backyard and toward her porch. Flickering light shone around the edges of the curtain covering the window in the backdoor; Mrs. Jackson must still be watching television inside. Well, they hadn't been gone very long. Not nearly long enough.

Samson, you and I are going to have a talk about your terrible timing.

When they stepped beneath the porch awning, Kelli beelined for the door as though she couldn't wait to get inside. He cast about for a reason to delay his departure. Should he say he was thirsty and ask for a drink of water? Maybe she'd invite him in.

She turned at the door. "Thank you for the walk, and for the furniture, and—" she gave him a quick smile "—everything. I'll see you in the morning."

Well, that was a dismissal if he'd ever heard one. The moment they'd shared in front of the bear enclosure was gone, a distant memory, and apparently she wasn't interested in repeating it. His spirits low at the thought, Jason nodded and turned to go.

"Wait." He whirled back toward her. "I have something for you." He dug in his pocket and pulled out the key ring he'd intended to give her.

Her eyebrows drew together as she stared at it. "What's this?"

He grasped one key between his finger and thumb. "This is the key to your house, the one you gave me." He dropped that one and selected the second. "And this is a key to the padlock on the zoo's rear gate. I thought it might be easier for you to just walk across the backyard." He grinned and lowered his voice. "Unless you think leaving the car here would be too big a temptation for your grandmother."

Kelli's lips parted as she stared at the keys. The look in the eyes she lifted to his made his heart do funny things, like he'd just given her the most precious gift in the world. Cool fingers grazed his palm as she took the keys. Then she leaned forward and, with a feather-light touch of soft lips, brushed a kiss on his cheek.

Then she disappeared into the house before he had recovered enough to stop her. He turned, trance-like, and headed back across the yard toward the zoo.

"Well, that wasn't as good as the one Samson preempted," he told the smattering of stars that had appeared in the swiftly darkening sky, "but it was a start." He touched his cheek with his fingertips and grinned. "A good start."

The bed linens smelled faintly of bleach and fabric softener. Kelli snuggled beneath the crisp white sheets and relished the feel of the pillow that fluffed around her head. This mattress was even more comfortable than hers at home. She made a mental note to pick up a thank-you card before she saw Barb at church Sunday. She and Nana could both sign it. That would be the nice thing to do.

And much safer than her thank-you kiss on Jason's cheek.

She nestled deeper in the pillow and pulled the comforter up around her chin. All evening long, she'd been unable to concentrate on anything because of that silly kiss. Her computer beckoned, but even though she tried to get some work done, she would come to herself with a start and realize she'd been staring at the screen, her mind a million miles away and her fingers absently rubbing her lips.

A thought struck her with the force of a slap, and she sat straight up in bed.

I'm falling for him.

All those protests to Nana over the past week that he was just a nice guy had been an attempt to convince herself as much as her grandmother. The truth was that Jason Andover was more than just a nice guy. He was dangerously handsome. Treacherously kind and understanding. Perilously considerate.

A soft moan escaped her clenched lips. She lifted her eyes to the ceiling and whispered in a voice so urgent it came out like a hiss. "Lord, how could this have happened? He's a zookeeper!"

Not only that, but Jason was her mother's handpicked replacement. A suspicion crept into her mind, and she cast a glare toward the doorway and Lillian's office beyond. Had her mother done this on purpose? Had she arranged her trust conditions with the hope that Kelli would fall in love with a zookeeper, as she had?

VIRGINIA SMITH

"Well, there's a long road between attraction and love," she informed the doorway. "And the only road trip I'm taking is back to Denver in five months and three weeks."

But the next few months would get awfully lonely with Nana as her only friend. For the past week she'd looked forward to sitting beside Jason and his mother in church, to blending her voice with his on the praise hymns the band played. To maybe going out to Sunday dinner with them after the service. She'd actually pictured herself talking to him about—well, about her past. After sixteen years of silence, she'd finally begun to hope she'd found someone who not only understood about zoos, but would also understand her side of the horrible incident. Maybe even help her sink that rusty car for good. Did she have to give up that hope?

Why can't we be friends? After all, I have to work with him every day. There's no way to avoid him completely.

She'd just have to be careful, that's all. No more romantic walks at night. That was off-limits. An unwelcome thrill shot through her at the memory of their almost-kiss by the bear enclosure. The stupid lion had done her a favor, actually.

As she settled herself back beneath the comforter and reached for the lamp, Leo stepped out from the closet.

"Well, hello there." Kelli kept her voice low. "Have you decided to forgive me for taking over your bedroom?"

Jason had moved the cat's toys, bed and climbing tree into the office, but apparently Leo was staging a revolt and refused to relocate. Kelli had found him curled up in the corner of the closet floor when she hung her clothes. He had not emerged all evening.

She expected Leo to run back into hiding, as he always did when she spoke. To her surprise, he walked into the room and sat in the middle of the floor, his tail curved neatly around his body. He fixed an unblinking stare on her.

"You're not running away from me." Maybe the cat missed her while she was gone. The thought brought an unbidden smile to Kelli's lips. She had no experience at all with animals, domestic or otherwise. But even though Leo was a feline, he wasn't at all threatening. In fact, he was kind of cute, with those white patches on his cheeks and the tips of his paws.

"You know, I'm only here temporarily. We could share this room, if you don't mind having a roommate."

Apparently Leo liked the suggestion. With one impressive leap, he jumped onto the bed. Kelli held her breath, afraid he'd run away if she moved. He sauntered the length of the mattress, close enough to rub against her leg as he went. When he got to the far end, he lowered himself into a sphinx-like pose beside her covered feet, his paws in front of him and his golden eyes turned her way.

"Well, I really meant I'd bring your bed back in here, but if you prefer the big one—" She turned off the lamp and settled deeply into the pillow. "I hope you don't snore."

Chapter Sixteen

Kelli sat at the shady end of a picnic table and listened to the zookeepers' banter as they ate their lunch. She'd spent the morning with Raul, who welcomed her back gruffly and then set her to work cleaning out the porcupine exhibit. No sign that he'd missed her during her absence, but he did allow her to feed Gasira and Baya big chunks of carrots by hand. The porcupines had been overjoyed, although Kelli suspected their enthusiasm had more to do with the carrots than with her.

She'd found the picnic table in the employees-only courtyard behind the office and was just finishing the sandwich Nana had made for her lunch when the others arrived. They'd called a casual welcome as they gathered around and unwrapped their own lunches.

Kelli ate the last bite and took her time wadding up the napkin and shoving it in the bag. Although she'd met most of the keepers the week of her mother's funeral, this was the first time she'd had lunch with them as a fellow zoo employee. She listened to their easy banter, enjoying the casual camaraderie that they extended to her.

The wooden privacy gate that led to the zoo's public area edged open and a figure slipped through. Kelli caught sight of a familiar flash of sun-kissed brown hair and straightened on the bench.

Erica, the short blonde who took care of the sheep, deer and peccaries, swiveled around to smirk in Jason's direction. "Hey, look who's decided to have lunch with the peons."

"Well, if it isn't Mr. Director," said Sherry, the keeper in charge of birds.

Michael, the cat keeper, made a show of unfolding a napkin and laying it across the bench beside him. "Here's your seat, boss. We'd hate for you to get dirt on your clothes in case you have to go to a meeting or something."

They all laughed, and Jason took the good-natured ribbing with a roll of his eyes. Kelli glanced around the table. That they all liked Jason was obvious by their easy smiles and teasing banter.

"Come on, you guys. You know better than that." He snatched up the napkin, wadded it in a ball and tossed it into Michael's lap before straddling the bench to face them. "I do have something serious to tell you, though."

Cameron moaned. "Don't tell me Westminster Academy Summer Camp is coming again. I'd rather deal with a hundred regular kids than five of those snobby rich brats any day."

Jason shook his head. "Worse, I'm afraid. We received a notice from AZA this morning. They're conducting an interim inspection for next Friday." He cast a quick glance in Kelli's direction. "They're specifically interested in seeing our shift procedures."

Several groans around the table met this news. Nobody else looked toward Kelli, but she wanted to sink beneath the table anyway. This inspection was her fault, and everyone knew it.

"It won't be that bad. We know what we're doing. We'll just show them how we do our jobs, that's all." Jason's expression displayed no anxiety at all, which seemed to calm the others.

"That's right." Michael faced Jason, but Kelli saw his eyes flicker briefly toward her. "Long as we all follow procedures, they're not going to find anything."

Cameron straightened. "I can shift Cocoa in and out all day long. We'll just need to make sure we have plenty of bananas on hand."

"You got 'em." Jason slapped him on the arm as he rose. He looked across the table. "Kelli, you're with me for the afternoon."

Blood roared in her ears. She thought she was supposed to train with Sherry or one of the other keepers she hadn't worked with yet. Was this an attempt to keep her close by, so she wouldn't do anything else to get the zoo in trouble?

Or just an attempt to keep her close by?

Heat flooded her face as she gathered the trash from her lunch. "What will we be doing?"

The smile that curved Jason's mouth had a false quality, as though he was assigning a particularly unpleasant task. "We're making piñatas."

Erica placed a sympathetic hand on her arm. "You poor thing."

The others gave her varying looks of pity as they nodded agreement.

Baffled, she looked from one to the other. "What's so bad about making piñatas?"

"You'll see," Michael told her as they all got to their feet.

Kelli disposed of her trash as the others dispersed, until finally she and Jason were the last to leave the courtyard. He held the gate open for her, and then walked silently beside her to the commissary. She tried to think of something to say that would restore the ease of last night's time together, but she found herself uncharacteristically tongue-tied.

When they arrived at the commissary building, Kelli found a huge stack of newspapers, a white plastic bucket and a giant bag of flour set out on the worktable.

She turned a surprised look on Jason. "When you said piñatas, I thought that was zoo jargon for something else. You mean piñatas?"

"Absolutely."

From a shelf against the rear wall, he reached down a storage bin. When he set it on the worktable, Kelli saw several packages of balloons and pots of paint inside.

"We have an enrichment program that encourages natural behaviors in our animals. It stimulates their physical and mental activity levels. That might include giving them toys, or introducing them to different objects." Jason turned a grin on her. "Cameron sometimes blows bubbles into the spider monkey's enclosure. You should see them trying to catch the bubbles."

Kelli resolutely ignored the thrill his grin caused. "So the piñatas are toys they play with?"

"Sort of. We also put food inside, which makes them think and work for their meal as they would in the wild. We'll make the piñatas in interesting shapes and fill them with whatever food each animal is permitted to have." He picked up one of the jars. "This paint is environmentally safe and harmless to the animals."

Kelli examined a package of balloons in a variety of sizes exactly like you'd buy for a child's party. "Interesting shapes, huh?"

"It can be anything, really." He returned the paint to the bin. "Some of the keepers get pretty creative, even make piñatas in the shape of the animals' natural prey."

"No kidding?" This might be fun, sort of like art class in grade school. Kelli tore into the plastic and extracted a round balloon. "Like a beehive for the bears to find honey in?"

He laughed. "Whatever you want."

Jason picked up a newspaper and a pair of scissors, and cut a long strand off with a smooth, practiced gesture. He nodded to indicate the empty place beside him, and Kelli slipped into it. She mimicked his actions, cutting paper strips and trying to ignore the fact that he stood just inches away.

"I don't see why everyone acted like this is such a terrible job." She spoke mostly to distract herself, because she kept imagining that all she had to do was edge sideways a tiny bit and their shoulders would touch.

Jason grinned down at her. "By the end of the day, you'll understand."

He was right. By six-thirty that evening, Kelli's arms felt like fifty-pound weights dragging on her poor, aching shoulders. Her hands had cramped around the scissors after an hour of cutting, and her fingers were raw from flour paste. But she had two dozen drying piñatas to show for her efforts.

Jason, who had left after giving careful instructions for the construction of piñatas, returned as she was rinsing out the paste bucket.

"Your workaholic tendencies are showing," he teased. "Quitting time was over an hour ago."

"Look!" She pointed proudly at one of her creations. "Do you know what that is?" She didn't wait for him to guess. "It's a giant bunch of bananas!"

Jason cast a skeptical eye toward the odd-looking shape in the center of the table. "It is?"

She nodded and picked it up gingerly so he could get a better look. "I glued several long balloons together and wrapped them and created a stem. Here's even some twine we can use to hang it from a tree branch."

His forehead wrinkled as he stared at her creation. "Aren't bananas supposed to be curved?"

Kelli thrust her nose into the air as she carefully set it back on the table. "Obviously you don't appreciate fine art. This is an impressionist's interpretation of bananas."

Humor twitched the corners of his mouth. "I'm sure Cocoa is much more of an art enthusiast than I. She'll love ripping into that." He glanced around the room and did a double-take at the trio of four-legged creatures standing in the corner. His eyebrows arched. "I'm impressed. Those deer are great, better than most efforts I've seen."

Kelli considered taking all the credit, but then admitted, "Erica came by right after you left and showed me how to make them. I'm particularly proud of the zebra."

He looked as though he was trying not to smile. "You know who'll get the zebra, don't you?"

She knew. With every stroke of her paintbrush, she'd been aware that zebras were the natural prey of lions. Perhaps it was telling that the zebra was the only animal-shaped piñata that was not wearing a painted-on smile. In fact, she'd paid special attention to his frown.

She inclined her head to Jason, but didn't answer.

"Well, excellent work. Really."

Despite herself, she preened at his compliment. "Thank you."

"And now do you understand why nobody wants to do piñatas?"

"Oh, I sure do." Kelli stretched her aching back. "I've never been so sore in my life." She rolled her shoulders in an effort to relieve the pressure.

"Here, let me help."

Jason had come up behind her, and before she knew what he intended, his hands were on her shoulders. Kelli froze. She should step away, put a stop to this right now. But before she could force herself to move, strong fingers began kneading the tension from her stiff muscles. A sigh of relief escaped her parted lips.

A faint voice whispered in her head. *This is exactly the kind of situation you should avoid.* She chose to ignore the warning and focused instead on Jason's hands coaxing the soreness away.

He's a zookeeper, just like Daddy.

Stiffening, she stepped forward, and his hands instantly dropped away. What was she thinking? She turned, her mouth open to say something to dispel the energy that seemed to vibrate in the air around them, though what she might say, she had no clue. She looked up, into Jason's eyes—

And in the next moment she was in his arms. Her traitorous lips rose to meet his, and the room dimmed around her at the touch of his feather-light kiss. The warning alarms sounding in her head receded to an easy-to-ignore whisper. Thank goodness for the sturdy worktable behind her; her wobbly knees would have dumped her on the floor for sure if she weren't leaning against it.

When he raised his head, his eyes danced. "From now on, piñatas will be my favorite job."

A battle raged in Kelli's heart. At this moment, with his arms wrapped around her and the masculine smell of him filling her nostrils, she felt like Jason could be the one she'd waited her whole life for. His lips had left hers only moments before, and already she longed for another kiss.

But he was a risk she couldn't take.

With a tremendous effort, she sidestepped away. "I can't do this, Jason."

His arms dropped to his side. "I don't understand. I'm attracted to you, Kelli, and unless I'm very much mistaken, you feel the same."

Not a word about love. Of course not. Nana was the only person who really loved her, the only one she could trust not to leave her. Everybody else abandoned her.

Kelli wrapped her arms around her middle and squeezed. "You're my boss. You'll probably lose your job if they find out you're—" she swallowed and lowered her eyes "—interested in one of your employees."

"Actually, I won't." He leaned a hip against the worktable. "I checked. There are no policies against employees dating. I guess that's because Cougar Bay was originally a private zoo, owned by a family. Everybody was related to everybody back then, so they never established any rules against it." He ducked his head in an attempt to catch her eye with a grin. "Though I'm sure we'll take a bit of ribbing from the others."

Kelli refused to look up. "I can't go out with you, Jason. I—I won't."

"Why?" His voice was soft. "It's because of whatever happened between you and Lil, isn't it?"

An invisible fist squeezed her throat shut. When she didn't answer, he went on.

"You mentioned you'd been traumatized. What happened, Kelli?" He placed a finger beneath her chin and gently lifted her face until she was looking into his eyes. "You can tell me."

Staring into those green-brown pools of compassion, Kelli felt that maybe she could. She opened her mouth, but no words came. Tears blurred her vision, and she looked away, shaking her head.

"I—I've got to go." Before he could stop her, Kelli whirled and ran from the building. She needed to get out of there, to get home.

And she didn't mean Lillian's house either.

Chapter Seventeen

The door slammed behind her, leaving Jason alone in a room full of paper-and-paste animals. The turmoil in his stomach kept his feet in place. Sure, he was attracted to her, but when he kissed her he wasn't expecting such a tidal wave of emotion to sweep over him. Over them both, judging by the way Kelli responded.

I don't need this, Lord. I've made one major mistake in my life already, and look what happened.

No, it was better to let her go. No matter what, he couldn't risk having another woman end up hating him. His glance fell on the yellow blob that was supposed to be a bunch of bananas. She'd sure been proud of that silly thing. He ran a finger over the still-wet paint and looked absently at the yellow stain on his skin.

But I'm not a wild college kid anymore. And Kelli is nothing like Aimee. She's determined, and professional, and smart, and beautiful and …

And he couldn't let her go.

What was he doing, standing here while she ran away? Like a shot, Jason was out the door, shouting.

"Kelli! Kelli, wait."

No sight of her in either direction. Which way had she run? She was heading for home, obviously. The shortest route to the back gate would have taken her right past the lion exhibit, so she would have chosen the long way. Maybe he could cut her off.

Sprinting like a runner, he dashed down the neat path, past the bears and the cougars, and didn't even spare a glance toward Samson. The trails were empty, because the zoo closed at six-thirty, but he did zip by Michael performing his end-of-day check on the bobcat.

"Hey, Jason, what's going on?"

Jason lifted a hand in response, but didn't waste breath to answer. When he turned the corner, he scanned the path ahead of him without slowing. At the sight of Kelli, just turning from the trail that led to the Small Animal building, he kicked into high speed.

"Kelli, stop!"

She ignored him, and for a moment he thought he'd have to chase her all the way to her house. But when she reached the back gate, she finally came to a halt. Jason skidded to a stop beside her, panting.

Disheveled brown hair fluttered around her shoulders like a glossy curtain. Her gaze fixed on the padlock, she lifted a hand to wipe a tear from her cheek. "I forgot my purse with the key in it."

Jason was torn between the desire to grab her and shake her for running away, or brush the tear from the other cheek. To keep from touching her, he shoved his hands into his pocket and pulled out his own key ring.

"I have one. But first, you have to tell me why you ran."

Her shoulders deflated and she half turned toward the direction she'd just come from. "I'll go get my purse."

He stepped in front of her to block her escape. "Please don't go. Talk to me, Kelli."

She didn't answer, but at least she didn't run away from him. Encouraged, he pressed his advantage. "Look at me." Hesitantly, her chin lifted. The delicate skin around her eyes was puffy from crying. "You can trust me."

Clear gray eyes searched his, probing more deeply than a blade. When she gave a slow, single nod, Jason expelled the breath he'd been holding. He gestured toward a bench nestled among the thick flowering hedge. When they were seated, she kept her head facing straight ahead, into the kangaroo yard, although from her unspoken stare her thoughts were far away from the napping marsupials. Jason resisted the temptation to drape his arm across the back of the bench. Instead, he sat beside her, not touching her, his body turned so he could watch her profile as she talked.

"I don't really know where to start. How much did my mother tell you about her past?"

Jason shook his head. "Almost nothing."

A shadowy smile flashed onto her face and disappeared just as quickly. "I figured that, since nobody here even knew I existed. She met my father right after she got out of college, when she took her first job as a zookeeper." Her gaze flickered toward him. "He trained her."

Just like Jason was training Kelli. He nodded, but held his tongue.

"They dated for five years before they got married." She stopped, shook her head. "No, I doubt if they ever really dated. They worked together. The zoo was their life, their focus. Daddy's specialty was exotic cats, and Mother's was primates." A real smile, small but genuine, curved her lips. "When I came along, I was raised right alongside the chimpanzees. After I was in school, I was the envy of all my classmates because I got to go to the zoo every day." The smile turned sour. "I had to, if I wanted to see either of my parents."

Jason shifted his weight and propped a leg across his knee. She'd just answered one of his questions. Since Kelli's last name was different from her mother's, he'd wondered if maybe Lil and Kelli's father had not been married. Now that he thought about it, Lil was independent in the extreme. It would be natural for her to keep her maiden name.

"So both your parents were workaholics." He teased her with their ongoing joke to coax the smile back to her face.

It didn't work. Her throat moved as she swallowed before continuing. "I went to work with them on the weekends, too. One Saturday when I was eight years old, I was following Daddy around while he worked. It was early in the morning, so the zoo wasn't open yet. He went into the lion's cage to clean it."

The change in her tone made Jason's stomach tense. This was it, the trauma she'd hinted at. Horror stole over Jason. He knew what was coming. *Oh, Lord, that poor little girl.*

Her head tilted forward as she stared at her tightly clasped hands, tormented by a long-ago memory. "I don't know what happened. Somehow the door the lion was behind came open while Daddy was inside. He—" She squeezed her eyes shut, and Jason watched a tear slide from between her eyelids. "He was killed."

Automatically, Jason leaned over and pulled her toward him with a protective arm around her shoulders. "While you watched."

She didn't resist his embrace, but leaned into it. Her head nodded against his shoulder. "It was … horrible. I screamed and screamed, but by the time anybody heard me it was too late to save him." A shudder ripped through her body, and Jason pulled her tighter. "My mother was the first person to get there."

Jason shut his eyes, but couldn't block out the scene that unfolded in his imagination. It was one he'd pictured before. Several years ago, when he was still in school. "Was your father David Jackson?"

"You've heard of him?"

"I have." He'd never connected the names, but every person associated with the care of exotic animals had heard of David

Jackson and the horrible lion attack that took his life. Even though the incident had occurred sixteen years ago, one of Jason's university professors had described it in detail as a somber warning to her students who planned to pursue a career caring for exotic animals. Of course, there had been no mention of David Jackson's young daughter's presence during the attack.

No wonder Lil had never mentioned her husband. A private person like Lil would hate the sort of attention that would bring.

Kelli straightened, pulling away from him, and scrubbed at her wet eyes with a sniff. "I had nightmares for years." Her shoulders jerked with a humorless laugh. "Still do, every so often."

"I can understand that. It was a horrible thing for a child to witness."

"Of course I had counseling, years of it. But I could never go back to the zoo." She wiped her hands on her slacks. "You can imagine how my mother felt about that."

Disbelief stole over Jason, stiffening his spine. "Do you mean she stayed at that zoo? Even after her husband was killed there?"

Kelli's lips twisted. "Not only that, but a few months later she insisted on being transferred to the cats. Of course, the lion that killed my father was put down after the attack, but she took care of the one that replaced him."

Jason could only stare at Kelli, speechless. Every day Lil had gone into the cage where her husband died, cleaned the floor, refreshed the water. Performed the same actions he'd performed moments before his death. What kind of twisted person would do that?

Kelli must have seen the question on his face. Her expression softened and she placed a hand on his arm. "It took me years to understand why. Exotic cats were his passion, so maybe caring for them made her feel closer to him. Plus, I think that was her therapy, in a way. Sort of like people who forgive someone who murdered their loved one. She found some sort of personal healing in forgiving the animal who killed her husband."

That made sense. Suddenly Lil's request made sense, too. "I suppose she wanted you to find that same healing. That's the reason for the six months working here."

"I suppose so." Her expression became hard again. "Frankly, at times I think it would be easier to forgive that lion than the mother who sent me away when I needed her the most."

Everything became clear as the last tumbler slipped into place. "She sent you to live with your grandmother because she couldn't stand to leave the zoo, and you couldn't stand to stay there."

Kelli nodded. "Her job was more important to her than her daughter." She turned on the bench so she was facing him, and her chin thrust forward. "So now you know why I can't fall in love with a zookeeper."

His pulse stuttered. Was Kelli falling in love with him? Sudden joy ballooned inside him with the thought. Was it possible? With an intensity that almost robbed him of breath, he wished for that to be true.

Lord, I've got to tell her about Aimee. And Tiffany.

But not right now. She'd just opened her life to him, invited him to see a past she'd never shared with anyone else. If he was going to have any chance to win her heart—and he knew with a fierce certainty that he desperately wanted to do just that—he needed to help her overcome the terrible trauma she'd experienced.

Moving slowly, afraid she'd run away if he didn't tread gingerly, he reached for her hand. Encouraged when she didn't resist, he enfolded it in his.

"It's an obstacle, I'll grant you that. But I think it's one we can overcome."

"You don't understand." She shook her head and started to pull away, but he gripped her hand tighter.

"I do understand, Kelli. I really do. But my mom always says there is no mountain too big for God to move. How about if we both agree to let Him handle this one?"

A tiny flame of hope flickered in her eyes. "I am from Colorado, you know. I've climbed lots of mountains."

"Well, there you go." He leaned forward, encouraged when she didn't back away from him. "And this time you won't be climbing alone."

Their kiss, soft as a whisper, strengthened Jason's resolve. He'd never been one to pray as often as he should, but that was about to change. Their situation was serious. He was a zookeeper, just like her father and the mother who had hurt her so deeply. Her reluctance to fall in love with him was entirely understandable. But zoology was the only thing he knew. He'd never held a job outside of a zoo, had never wanted to. The mountain between them really did seem insurmountable.

But this was one woman he didn't intend to let slip away. Somehow, they would figure out a way to be together.

Lord, You're about to start hearing from me on a regular basis.

Chapter Eighteen

The world was a brand-new place in the morning. Her sleep had been sweetened with dreams of Jason, and she'd awoken with a full heart and fresh determination. Why should she continue to crouch in the shadows of the past, when the future could be bathed with sunlight?

A future with Jason? Could she actually move away from Denver, leave her job there? As she let herself through the zoo's back gate, she turned a smile upward, toward the bright Florida sun. Maybe, if Nana came with her. After all, Florida needed accountants, too. With Lillian's trust money, she could set up her accounting firm here as well as there.

With a light step, she bounced along the path to the Small Animal building to let Raul know she'd be in the commissary this morning, finishing up her piñatas. She even smiled at his gruff grunt of dismissal.

When she arrived at the commissary, Erica was already at work shoving food through the openings she'd left in the top of each of her creations.

The girl looked up as she entered. "Hey. Jason grabbed me on the way in and asked me to show you how to stuff them."

Kelli stopped short. "Oh." If she'd known he wasn't going to be here, she would have stopped by the office on her way, just to say good morning.

"He said something about an early phone conference with somebody from the AZA." Erica grimaced. "Probably about the inspection next week."

Kelli stepped up to the table, picked up an object that looked roughly like a giant pineapple and started inserting the pile of chopped produce Erica had already prepared. "Have you been through an inspection before?"

"Yeah, it's not a big deal. They'll probably spend some time looking through the written procedures, then they'll come around and check out the animals, talk to the keepers." She shrugged as she fed two raisins at a time through the small opening of an orange orb. Then she gave Kelli a kind smile. "Don't worry about it. It'll be fine."

Kelli hid a grimace. So everyone *did* know that she was the cause of the special inspection.

Filling the piñatas took several hours. When they were finished, Kelli washed her hands, which smelled of the raw meat for the carnivores, while Erica put out a call over the radio. In a few minutes, keepers started arriving to pick up piñatas for their charges.

Kelli's pulse quickened when Jason stepped through the door behind Michael and Cameron. A slow smile stole across his face when he caught sight of her, which sent an answering shaft of warmth through her.

"Good morning." His greeting, uttered in a voice low enough to be a purr, blotted out everything else in the room. Kelli's heart hammered in her chest as she managed a breathless "Good morning" in return.

The exclamations of the others intruded on their private moment. Reluctantly, Kelli turned her attention to them.

"Great job," Sherry congratulated her.

Cameron held up the bananas for inspection. "You should have seen my first piñatas. They were shaped like lopsided balloons. This is terrific."

Kelli turned a triumphant smile on Jason. "At least someone around here appreciates art."

Jason rolled his eyes with a good-natured grin. "Since you're so good at it, we'll give you the job of official piñata maker, if you're interested."

Hands held up as if to ward off the terrible suggestion, Kelli made a show of backing away from him while everyone laughed.

"Come with me, Kelli," Cameron told her. "Cocoa is going to love this."

She glanced at Jason, and he nodded. "That's the best part of making piñatas—watching the animals' reactions."

They all got rolling carts out of a storage room and loaded Kelli's creations. Outside the commissary, the group split up. Kelli hid her smile when Jason joined her and Cameron on their way to the orangutan exhibit.

Cocoa was inside, lying on the floor in the far corner, her back to the glass. No shows for her admiring audience on this lazy morning. Kelli and Jason followed Cameron to a nearby workroom to retrieve an extension ladder, then helped him carry it through a series of access doors into the ape's moated yard. A crowd gathered in the viewing area as Cameron carefully positioned the ladder and then fixed the bright yellow object in a high branch.

There was no window looking from the orangutan's indoor enclosure to the outdoor exhibit, so Cocoa couldn't see where they hid the treasure. She stirred as they exited the yard, apparently alerted by the slamming of the gates. Kelli watched the animal heft herself to her feet and wander lazily to the closed access panel, then seat herself in front of it, prepared to wait patiently for it to open.

When the inside door had been closed and bolted, Cameron pulled a thick rope that slid open the panel.

"Come on. Let's go outside and watch." Jason put a hand on her back and guided her out of the small access room.

They joined the group in the viewing area and took up positions behind several children so they could see over their heads.

"She don't see it," one boy complained. He cupped his hands around his mouth and called down into the enclosure, "Hey monkey, look up!"

The other kids joined in the effort, and the air filled with high-pitched shouts urging Cocoa toward the piñata. Cocoa did not acknowledge them at all, but made her leisurely way across the grass and climbed up to her platform. Kelli watched, marveling at the way the orang managed to look regal, as though the screaming crowd wasn't worth her notice. She was fully aware of the people, but apparently wasn't in the mood for antics today.

Until she caught sight of the piñata. Her reddish-brown form straightened, her gigantic head tilted upward. In a flash, she was off the platform, climbing high up the tree where the piñata was suspended. The children let out a collective *ooh* when she started to hand-walk across the branch that bent precariously under her weight. Apparently, Cocoa decided the branch wouldn't hold her and backed up.

The little boy who'd first shouted turned a concerned look up at Jason, who stood behind him. "She can't reach it."

Kelli had been just about to voice the same concern, but Jason's expression displayed complete confidence. "She'll get it. Just watch."

Cocoa backed up toward the trunk and dropped down to the sturdier branch below. She edged outward, and when the branch started to bend, she twisted around so she stood on it, her agile toes holding as tight as fingers. She reached up and grabbed the higher branch, inched outward a little farther, then bent the top branch downward with one long-fingered hand while she stretched for the piñata with the other. The children cheered when she grasped the yellow object.

"What is that thing, anyway?" asked a girl as the orang made her way back to her platform, her prize clutched in her hand.

"It's just a big yellow blob," answered her friend with a superior nod.

Laughter hovered in the look Jason turned toward Kelli, and she couldn't help chuckling herself. Apparently she and Cameron were the only ones who recognized her *objet d'art*.

"It's part of our enrichment program," said Cameron, who had just joined them. Then he launched into an explanation of the zoo's program. His audience listened as they watched Cocoa settle back on her platform and plunge her fingers into the opening.

A feeling of satisfaction settled deep inside Kelli as she watched. She'd worked hard yesterday, but seeing the animal work to obtain the prize and her determination to uncover the goodies inside made the effort worthwhile. She became aware that Jason was staring at her, a teasing twinkle in his eyes.

"Apparently Cocoa is an art lover, too."

Kelli couldn't help saying, "I knew she would be."

He tilted his head back and laughed. When his laughter died away, his expression became sober. He looped a hand through her arm and pulled her away from the crowd. "How about watching another animal enjoy your work?"

A leaden lump dropped into Kelli's stomach. No question at all which animal he meant. She opened her mouth to refuse, but then stopped. This might be her first steps up the mountain they'd talked about last night. If she wanted to have a relationship with Jason, she had to at least get to the point where she could walk past the lion's exhibit without lapsing into hysterics. Hadn't she stayed up late into the night, praying for strength to overcome her fear?

Jason watched the struggle that must be apparent on her face, his gaze piercing. His hand slipped down her arm to squeeze her fingers. "If you don't want to, it's okay."

Her mouth dry as terry cloth, she managed to squeak an answer. "I don't want to. But I will."

Her reward was a blinding smile that dispelled the chill creeping over her. At least part of it.

"Good girl."

He didn't release her hand as they walked down the path Kelli had managed to avoid until now. Normally, she would have enjoyed strolling down the sidewalk, hand in hand with him, but every step took them closer to the object of more nightmares than she could count. Dread settled in her stomach. A bobcat, sitting in the sun inside its enclosure, turned its head to watch them pass, black-rimmed pointed ears at attention.

A small crowd stood in a cluster in front of the lion's exhibit. Jason didn't join them, but led her instead to stand some distance away, within view of the exhibit's interior but not right up against the protective fence that served as the first barrier. Kelli gave his hand a grateful squeeze, but couldn't manage to squeak a word through her dry mouth. The lion was nowhere in sight, but Michael was inside the enclosure, setting the zebra-shaped piñata in place. Tension knotted Kelli's insides as she watched him duck beneath the branches of a thick, smooth-sided artificial tree that looked like a grotesquely oversized version of Leo's climbing pole at home. The keeper sidestepped around a huge boulder and set the zebra up so its sad face peeked around the rock. A panel in the back wall rattled, and Kelli's heart thudded at the ominous sound. The lion wanted back in his cage.

"Samson is almost four years old." Jason's soft, even tone attempted to soothe her racing pulse as he recited facts about the feline as though he were just another zoo animal and not a ferocious killer. "Cougar Bay got him a year and a half ago, after the previous lion died of old age. He's fully mature and extremely healthy. He's been approved for breeding."

Kelli nodded, her eyes fixed on Michael as he worked. That explained Lillian's bequest to the zoo. "You're hoping to build that new Lion Habitat and get a female."

"That's right. Plus—"

Kelli tore her eyes away from the exhibit. "Plus what?"

Jason looked down at the ground between his feet, obviously uncomfortable. "Lil loved this lion. She wanted to see him out of that confined space and into someplace where he can move about freely."

Kelli's lips tightened and she bit back a sarcastic response. Yes, her mother loved this lion. All lions. She looked back at the enclosure. Although she had no expertise in such things, even she could see that this exhibit was pretty small for a large animal. Even with the sturdy-looking tree to climb, there wasn't much exercise room.

Inside the exhibit, Michael had finished placing the piñata and made his way to the door in the side wall. Only when he'd gone through it and closed the door behind him, taking him out of the danger zone, did Kelli's muscles relax.

But in the next moment, she tensed again. The back panel slid open with a loud rattle. Through the opening came the stuff of her nightmares. She sucked in a breath and fought to reject the images of horror her memory supplied. Only when Jason covered her hand with his and squeezed did she realize she'd grasped his arm in a death grip. She couldn't manage an apology, but did loosen her grip enough so that her nails wouldn't draw blood.

The lion that attacked her father had rushed, but this one didn't. Samson paced through the doorway, his giant paws treading silently on the concrete floor. Instead of coming into the center of his enclosure, he paced the perimeter to the corner in a well-traveled path, turned, and then headed to the front. At the door Michael had gone through, he paused, then turned to head back in the direction he'd just come, his great head moving as he surveyed his domain.

Then he spied the piñata.

He froze, statue-like except for the twitching tip of his tail, his gaze fixed on the black-and-white striped object. Kelli watched, fascinated in spite of herself, as he lowered his great body and began to inch slowly forward in a crouch.

"He's stalking it," she whispered.

Jason nodded. "Just like he'd do in the wild."

Actually, Kelli realized, he looked like Leo with a toy mouse she'd tossed into the corner just this morning. In fact, this gigantic cat bore a remarkable resemblance to her shy feline roommate. The way he held his tail rigid while he stalked, for instance, and the hunkered-down stoop of his shoulders.

When Samson reached the zebra, he didn't pounce, as she expected him to. Instead, he slowly extended his neck until he stood nose-to-nose with it. The click of cameras was the only noise from the watching crowd as the lion inspected the piñata, sniffing its legs and torso with increasing interest.

"He smells the meat inside," Kelli said.

She saw Jason's nod of assent in her peripheral vision, because she couldn't tear her eyes away from the lion. In fact, she realized with a start that she was eager to see how Samson intended to get at his treat. Her heart was no longer pounding with fear. Not that she intended to go any closer than this to the creature, certainly not into that cage to clean or anything else, but it was as satisfying to see Samson enjoy her piñata as it had been to watch Cocoa.

She turned her head to tell Jason when the radio clipped to his belt erupted with static. A second later, Angela's voice came through.

"Does anyone know where Kelli Jackson is working today?"

Startled, Kelli watched as Jason unclipped the radio and held it up to his mouth. "She's with me right now. Why?"

"We just got a call from the lady who lives across the street from Lil's house. Her grandmother's had an accident. There's an ambulance on the way."

Kelli's heart slammed to a stop. Nana!

If anything happens to Nana …

She couldn't finish the thought. Icy panic surged through her veins as she sprinted toward the back gate.

Chapter Nineteen

The chairs in the hospital waiting room were hard, plastic and as orange as the piñata Kelli had made for the spider monkeys. Only dingier. Jason shifted his weight, trying to ease the pressure of sitting in one place for over an hour. He would have gotten up and paced, but Kelli clutched his hand like a lifeline, and he didn't want to let go. He'd stay in place as long as she needed him.

"It's been over an hour since she went into surgery." Kelli's voice quivered. "Shouldn't the surgeon have come out by now? You don't think something went wrong, do you?"

Jason squeezed her hand. "They said the break to the femur was a bad one. The doctor is just taking his time, being thorough."

She nodded, her eyes fixed on the clock mounted on the wall in front of her, lips moving though no sound came out. Praying, as she'd done since they arrived. Jason did the same, lifting a silent plea to God for Mrs. Jackson's health. Although he would never suggest it to Kelli, he worried about the stamina of an eighty-one-year-old woman undergoing major surgery. What if she didn't survive?

Kelli burst out in an agonized voice, "Why was she trying to scrape paint off those stupid shutters, anyway? What possessed her to do that?"

"You heard her in the emergency room. She was just reaching over from the front porch to knock off the biggest chips. She leaned too far and lost her balance." Jason kept his tone even, a calming counterpoint to hers that bordered on panic. "It's a good thing the lady across the street saw her fall, or she might have lain there for hours."

A blue-garbed man bustled into the room. The surgeon still wore the surgery cap on his head and paper coverings on his shoes.

Kelli shot out of the chair and crossed the room fast as a cheetah. "How is she? Is she okay?"

Jason heaved a relieved sigh when the doctor smiled.

"She's fine. They just wheeled her into recovery." His expression sobered. "It was a bad break, though, one the most extensive procedures I've performed. We've inserted a rod and bolts to hold her bone in place while she heals, but given her age—" He shook his head.

"But she'll recover, right?" Kelli clasped her hands beneath her chin. The pleading look in her eyes brought Jason closer to her side to encircle her shoulders with a protective arm.

"Ms. Jackson, you need to understand that this has been a life-altering injury. She's eighty-one years old. Her body won't heal as well as it would have twenty years ago."

Tears choked Kelli's voice. "You mean she won't ever walk again?"

"Oh, I think she will. In time. But maybe not without the aid of a walker. When you choose a facility, make sure they have good rehab services."

"Facility?" Her eyes went round. "You mean she can't come home?"

"Is her house all on one level? Or at least have a bedroom and bathroom on the main floor so she doesn't have to go up and down stairs?"

Her teeth appeared and bit down on her lower lip. She glanced at Jason. "The one here in Florida is."

The doctor seemed to consider this. "She's going to need twenty-four-hour care for several weeks. I really think a good facility is the best option."

"I don't want Nana going into a nursing home." Kelli's chin shot upward. "I can take care of her."

His expression became kind. "Ms. Jackson, I'm sure you're willing. But she's elderly and her body has experienced a major trauma. It would be best if she were surrounded with people who are medically trained. You want what's best for your grandmother, don't you?"

Kelli's eyes flooded as she nodded.

Her tears stirred emotions inside Jason that he had never felt before. He wanted to protect her, to solve all her problems so she would never cry again.

An idea occurred to him. He squeezed Kelli's shoulders. "I'll be right back. I need to make a phone call."

Nana's face looked pasty and pale, nearly the same color as the pillow she lay propped against. Seeing her like this kept Kelli's stomach muscles knotted, although she forced herself to smile calmly as she held the bent straw to her grandmother's lips.

She continued outlining the arrangements as Nana sipped the ice water. "So Jason's mom said she would love to have you stay with her for a few weeks when you come home from the hospital. The doctor will arrange for Home Health to come in three times a week to check on you and make sure you're progressing like you should."

"But she doesn't know me at all. Why would she want to take care of a complete stranger?" Her drink finished, Nana collapsed against the pillow. "Maybe I'd better just go ahead and move into a nursing home now and get it over with. That way I won't be a burden to anyone."

Kelli covered her hand. "You're not a burden. And Barb is a very nice lady whose husband died not long ago. She nursed him full-time for several years, and she says she's been so bored since he passed away that she's even considered volunteering at the hospital just so she'll feel useful again." She gave Nana's hand a final pat and straightened. "She says you're an answer to her prayers."

When Jason told Kelli of his mother's offer, she'd cried with relief. It was the perfect solution to their problem.

A tiny smile crept across Nana's creased lips. "I've never been the answer to anyone's prayers before."

Emotion swept over Kelli, bringing a rush of fresh tears to her eyes. She leaned forward and gathered Nana into a gentle hug. "Oh, yes, you have. Mine."

She straightened, and Nana studied her through narrowed eyes for a moment. "Jason certainly has proven himself a knight in shining armor, hasn't he?"

Warmth crept up Kelli's neck. She smoothed a wrinkle from the white blanket. "He did come to our rescue."

"Am I to understand you've begun to consider your boss in a different role?"

"Perhaps." Nana's shrewd smile sent the blush into Kelli's cheeks. "I mean, he still has one big black mark against him. He does work in a zoo."

Nana's veiny hand crept across the blanket to stroke Kelli's arm. "That will be very difficult for you. Are you sure you want to date someone in that profession?"

Kelli avoided her gaze. "I think so."

"If he makes you happy, Kelli, that's the most important thing." With a final pat on Kelli's arm, Nana pulled the blanket higher under her chin. "I was thinking this morning before I fell that the warm weather here in Florida suits me far better than those harsh Colorado winters."

Her eyes took on a glimmer of their trademark twinkle, which untied a few of the knots in Kelli's stomach. With a chuckle, she shook a finger in Nana's direction. "Don't get any ideas just yet. There's no need to rush into anything."

But Nana's words sent her spirits soaring like a helium balloon. The reasons to return to Denver were all fading away one at a time. Jason's heart-stopping grin loomed in her mind's eye. Florida was looking less like a six-month assignment every minute.

Chapter Twenty

Jason stood beside Kelli, watching Michael work with Samson. The young keeper stood in the wide walkway between the waist-high public barrier and the sturdy metal mesh wall that formed the front of the lion's exhibit. Jason was impressed that Kelli had agreed to stand this close, just on the other side of the public barrier, not ten feet away from the animal. She'd schooled her expression into one of detached attention. If he hadn't been standing close enough to feel her tremble, he wouldn't guess she felt anything other than impersonal interest in the procedure.

Michael pressed the target, a bright green tennis ball on the end of a long pole, next to the fencing up high enough that Samson had to rise on his hind legs to touch his nose to it.

"Target, Samson."

The lion rose obediently and placed giant paws against the metal. Kelli, her eyes wide as Frisbees, jerked with a start as the metal mesh rattled.

Jason spoke in a low, calm voice. Maybe if he described the reason for the training exercise, it would distract her from her fear. "We train all the animals to a target like this, so we can get close enough to inspect them. When Michael has Samson rise up like that, he's checking his underbelly and paws to make sure there are no cuts or sores."

Michael acknowledged Samson's obedience with a short blast on the whistle he wore around his neck, and rewarded him with a chunk of meat shoved through the holes. After Samson had eaten the treat, Michael held the target out at arm's length, and the cat turned sideways to press his golden body against the welded mesh.

"That's so we can give him injections if we need to," Jason explained.

Her throat convulsed, but when she spoke, her voice matched his calm tone. "You don't tranquilize him? Like when Pete wants to give him a physical?"

"It's dangerous to tranquilize any animal. We only do it when we absolutely have to."

She nodded, her gaze fixed on Michael. "What about—"

Her question went unspoken. Samson, apparently tired of the training session, began an impossibly low and ominous growl, his big, golden eyes locked onto Michael. The sound reached a crescendo with an impressive roar that resonated in Jason's sternum and sent instinctive alarm signals speeding to his brain. He could hardly blame Kelli for running.

He dashed after her, Michael's voice fading behind him as he admonished the lion, "If you don't want to play anymore, fine. No need to get nasty about it."

Jason found Kelli around the corner, standing on the sidewalk with her arms wrapped around her middle and tears streaming down her face. Wordlessly, he gathered her in an embrace and held her tight while she heaved with quiet sobs.

"I can't do it, Jason." Her voice was muffled against his shirt. "I can't. I'll work here for five and a half more months. I'll make piñatas and clean cages all day long, but please don't ask me to go near that animal."

"Shhh. It's okay." He stroked her silky hair and hugged her tighter. "You don't have to."

She pulled back. Her hands balled into fists at her side. "This is all my mother's fault! If she were here right now, I'd—I'd shake her until her teeth rattled!"

"Kelli." He pitched his voice low. "I will be the first one to agree that your mom made some terrible mistakes. But what happened to your dad wasn't Lil's fault."

She wore an expression as fierce as Samson's had been moments ago. She spoke through gritted teeth. "If she had supported me instead of shipping me off to Colorado, I might have gotten over the trauma. But no, she was too busy taking care of another lion to worry about her only daughter. And another lion after that, and then—" she glared in the direction of Samson's cage "—that one!"

Anger flashed in her eyes, and the sight of it settled a sense of discomfort deep in Jason's core. He'd seen anger like that before—in Aimee's face, when she accused him of ruining her life. Would Kelli end up bitter and angry like Aimee?

He crushed her to him, trying to banish the thought. "You have to forgive her, Kelli. Not for Lil, but for yourself. Don't let your anger with your mother make you bitter."

At first she stood rigid in his arms, but after a moment, he felt her relax. "You're right. I know you are." She pulled away slightly to lift a weak smile up at him. "How did you get to be so wise?"

Now was the time to tell her about his past—and about Tiffany. "I've made mistakes of my own, mistakes that hurt others." Outrage flashed onto her face and she opened her mouth to speak, but he stopped her with a finger on her lips. "I'm not excusing Lil for choosing her career over you. It's just that I know what it's like to—"

Angela's voice erupted through his radio. "Jason, Francine Cowell is on the phone for you. Are you close enough to come to the office and talk to her?"

Frustrated, Jason pressed his lips tight. He couldn't have this conversation with Kelli right now. They needed to go someplace without the worry of interruptions.

He unclipped the radio from his belt. "Tell her I'll call her back in ten minutes." To Kelli he said, "She's a board member, so I need to talk to her. There's something I need to tell you, but this isn't the time or place. You're off work tomorrow to take your grandmother home from the hospital. What are you doing tomorrow evening?"

"I'd planned to spend the whole day at your mother's helping Nana get settled. After that—" She shrugged. "Go home and play with the cat, probably." Her gaze turned shy. "Unless I get a better offer."

Jason grinned. "You have one. Let's go to dinner. I'll pick you up around seven. Sound good?"

A warm glow lit her eyes. "Perfect."

As he made his way to the office and his phone call with Mrs. Cowell, he was already planning where they'd go on their first official date.

Chapter Twenty-One

"There you are, Mrs. Jackson. How did that feel?"

The physical therapist from Home Health stood beside the bed in Barb Andover's house, smiling down on Nana. She'd just demonstrated how to swing the injured leg from the floor to the mattress using the other leg as a lever. Kelli could tell the girl's overly-perky attitude was starting to irritate Nana, who grimaced with pain every time her leg moved.

"It felt like someone was sawing through my bone with a table knife, that's how it felt." Nana's normally cheerful disposition was nowhere in evidence as she collapsed backward on the pillows in the hospital bed.

Barb, standing beside Kelli in the doorway to her guest room, wore a sympathetic grimace. "I'll help Mrs. Jackson work on that after she's had a nap. This has been an exhausting day for all of us."

Kelli turned a grateful smile toward Jason's mother. Barb had been the epitome of kindness throughout the afternoon, ever since Nana and Kelli arrived from the hospital.

"That will be perfect," the therapist said, with too much enthusiasm. She placed a hand on Nana's arm and directed a slightly louder voice to her elderly patient. "I'll be back to see you on Friday, Mrs. Jackson. You practice getting in and out of bed on your own, and we'll move on to something else then."

Nana didn't open her eyes as she answered in a voice dripping with sarcasm. "I'll be counting the days."

"That's the spirit!" The clueless girl beamed down on her
patient.

Kelli and Barb both hid a smile as the therapist gathered her
papers and left. Barb walked her to the front door, while Kelli
moved to Nana's bedside.

"She's a little hard to take, isn't she?" She kept her voice low.

Nana cracked an eye and glanced around the room, as
though assuring herself the girl was really gone. "I half expected
her to pull out her pom-poms and give me a cheer for making it
all the way from the wheelchair to the bed." Her eyes shut again.
"Which I hate using, by the way."

"I know." Kelli placed a sympathetic hand on her arm.
"But it's only temporary, until you can walk farther than two
feet without collapsing. If you work hard at those exercises she
showed you—"

Nana's deep breathing alerted Kelli to the fact that she had
fallen asleep. The day had been exhausting for her. Moving
silently, Kelli tiptoed from the room and pulled the door shut
behind her. A monitor on the nightstand beside the bed would
alert her and Barb if Nana woke and called for them.

Barb really did have a perfect setup to care for an invalid,
although Kelli felt slightly guilty that Nana would occupy the
master suite while Barb slept in one of the smaller bedrooms
on the opposite side of the house. But Barb explained that she'd
become comfortable in the cozy bedroom, where she'd moved
her furniture when the necessity for a hospital bed for her husband had arisen. Prior to that, the room had held the white-and-
gold daybed Kelli was sleeping on.

A third bedroom, next door to Barb's, had been Jason's during childhood. Kelli crept down the hallway and peeked inside
the darkened room. Apparently, he'd been a sports fan. A baseball

bat and glove hung from a wooden stand on the wall, beneath an Atlanta Braves pennant. On the other wall was a framed picture of a tall basketball player beside a preteen boy. She could just see the dark scrawl of a signature in the lower corner of the picture. Kelli wanted to slip inside and study the boy's face, but she hated for Barb to catch her snooping around Jason's bedroom. With regret, she continued down the hallway to the kitchen, where she found Barb punching buttons on the microwave.

"There you are. I thought you might like a cup of herbal tea." She smiled and gestured for Kelli to be seated at the round table that dominated one corner of the room. "Is she sleeping?"

Kelli nodded as she slipped into a cushioned chair. "I think today has worn her out."

"Oh, I'm sure it has. Plus, major surgery is hard on anyone. I expect she'll sleep most of the time for the next few days."

She set a mug and spoon in front of Kelli and then arranged several boxes of herbal tea within reach. Kelli selected Apple Cinnamon Spice. "I want to thank you again. The way you gave her that shot in the stomach even impressed the Home Health nurse." Kelli shuddered. "I couldn't do it."

Barb dismissed her thanks with a wave. "That was nothing. I gave my husband injections for years. I'm sure your grandmother will be a dream. I really am looking forward to having someone to take care of."

The microwave beeped, and she pulled a steaming glass pitcher from it. She crossed the kitchen to Kelli's side and poured water on top of her tea bag. A cinnamony-apple fragrance rose with the steam, and Kelli inhaled deeply while Barb seated herself in the chair on the opposite side of the table.

"She really is a sweet person," Kelli said as she stirred a spoonful of sugar into the hot tea, "but today she's something of a crab."

"You should have seen Greg when he first started losing his independence. Now, there was a crab." Barb dunked her own tea bag up and down in her mug, her expression thoughtful. "Of course, becoming an invalid frustrated him so. I understood. And he always apologized after he'd snapped at me."

Compassion stirred in Kelli's heart. How awful it must have been to watch someone she loved deteriorate. And how lucky he was, to have someone like Barb. Unlike Lillian, who'd had no one to care for her at the end, except the nurses on staff at the hospital.

Kelli glanced around the kitchen for something to distract her from her disturbing thoughts. Her gaze fell on the refrigerator. It looked like Nana's in Denver, covered with handwritten reminders, to-do lists and snapshots. One picture stood out, perhaps because it was a close-up of a young child's laughing face, or maybe because it held a place of honor in the exact center of everything else. Even from this distance Kelli could see a family resemblance. The child's eyes were shaped like rounded almonds, exactly like Barb's, and framed with wispy sun-kissed brown bangs.

"What a pretty little girl." Kelli nodded toward the picture. "She's obviously related to you."

Barb twisted in her chair and glanced at the refrigerator. When she turned back around, she wore a wide smile. "Yes, she is. That's my granddaughter, Tiffany."

The smile on Kelli's face went cold. Granddaughter?

Barb lifted her tea bag and dangled it, dripping, above her mug, regret in the eyes that she kept fixed on the bag. "Tiffany just turned four, but I've only seen her twice. While Greg was alive I couldn't leave him long enough to visit her. So sad, really, because I missed playing with her as a baby."

Her mouth dry, Kelli lifted her mug and sipped the scalding tea. Even so, her voice cracked when she spoke. "I didn't realize you had children other than Jason."

Confusion creased Barb's brow. "I don't. Jason is our only son."

A dim buzz sounded in Kelli's ears as her blood picked up speed. "So Tiffany is Jason's—" She couldn't finish the sentence.

"He hasn't mentioned her?" A blush stained Barb's face. "I'm sorry. I shouldn't have said anything."

"Why not?" Kelli was horrified to hear her voice come out loud and sharp. "Is he ashamed of her?"

Barb leaned across the table, her hand outstretched. "Oh, no. Not of Tiffany. Of course not." She looked away, embarrassed. "But he probably is ashamed of his relationship with Tiffany's mother. You see, they were never married."

Jason had gotten a girl pregnant and hadn't married her. They had a child, a daughter. Was that child the *mistake* he was going to tell her about tonight?

Kelli gulped against the gathering anger that knotted her throat until she could speak evenly. "Tell me what happened."

The creases in Barb's forehead deepened. "I don't know if I should. Maybe you should talk to Jason."

"You know what?" Kelli stood, half-ashamed of the loud way the chair scooted across the linoleum behind her. "I think I will."

She recovered her composure enough to thank Barb again for coming to Nana's rescue, and to peek into the bedroom to assure herself that Nana was still sleeping. She even managed to smile into Barb's worried face before she left, promising to return later to check on Nana.

Once inside the car, she clutched the steering wheel with a white-knuckled grip. Jason had lied to her. Or, at the very least, deceived her. He had a *child* he hadn't bothered to tell her about. Or had his daughter just slipped his mind, because obviously she wasn't a priority in his life? Kelli's jaw clenched as her fury swelled like floodwaters. This was almost like Lillian, who hadn't bothered to tell anyone about her daughter. No, it was *exactly* like Lillian.

Well, Lillian was out of Kelli's reach now. But Jason wasn't.

Forcing herself to assume at least a semblance of calm so she wouldn't be a danger on the road, Kelli drove with exaggerated care toward the zoo. Just wait until she got her hands on Mr. Jason Andover.

Chapter Twenty-Two

Jason saved the file he'd been working on and closed the application. He'd satisfied himself that all the procedures on animal handling were up to date and ready for the inspectors Friday. The animal care staff was ready, too. Some of them were young, but even so, they were the best in the business. He'd stack Cougar Bay's keepers up against anyone, anywhere. There was no need to be anxious about this interim inspection. They'd sail through it with ease.

The door in the outer office slammed shut and he looked up to see Kelli enter. A rush of pleasure washed over him. He hadn't expected to see her until he picked her up for their dinner date.

At the fierce look on her face, his pleasure faded, along with the greeting he'd been about to voice. She stopped just inside his office, her eyes angry slits, her hands clenched into fists at her sides.

Uneasiness shafted through him. "What's wrong? Is your grandmother okay?"

She didn't acknowledge his question, but instead spoke in a deadly calm voice. "When were you planning to tell me about your daughter?"

Jason felt like a bug pinned to a velvet-covered board by her glare. With an effort, he crossed the two steps between them and reached for her arm to pull her farther inside the office.

She jerked out of his grasp with an indrawn breath, as though his touch burned. His lips tightened. Fine, if that's the way she wanted to play this. Moving with deliberate slowness, he closed the door. These walls weren't exactly soundproof, but at least they provided a semblance of privacy. And he had a feeling this discussion was going to be very, very private.

When he'd seated himself in his desk chair and gestured for Kelli to sit as well—which she ignored—he forced himself to match her fake-calm tone. "That was what I wanted to talk about tonight."

"So the big secret you were going to share, the *mistake*—" she spat the word "—was your daughter?"

"Of course not." He worked hard to maintain an even tone. Not easy in the face of her anger. "The mistake was a drunken week in Daytona Beach with some of my old college buddies a few years ago." He swallowed. This was not the way he'd planned to tell her about his jaded past. "Aimee was a sophomore at Embry-Riddle. I barely remembered meeting her until six weeks later when she called to tell me she was pregnant." His face burned, but he managed not to duck his head. "She wanted me to marry her, but I refused."

Kelli's eyes narrowed to slits. "Why?"

Jason placed both hands in his lap and returned Kelli's glare without flinching. "Because even though I wasn't a Christian at the time, I believed marriage was a sacred commitment. I didn't see how compounding one mistake with another would do either of us any good."

"So you dumped her. Left her with the responsibility of raising your child on her own."

He added a touch of volume to his voice. "I've supported Tiffany from day one."

"You mean you've paid child support? Excuse me for not giving you credit for doing everything the law *requires* you to do." Kelli folded her arms across her chest with a jerk. "How often do you see her?"

Now Jason did look away. "As often as I can. Once a month, if I'm able to get away from work. She lives two and a half hours away."

"Two and a half hours? You drove that long to deliver a couple of stupid monkeys to another zoo! You can't go to visit your own child more often than once a month?"

"You think it's easy to sit there in Aimee's living room with her glaring at me the whole time?" Appalled at the way his voice filled the tiny office, Jason resumed the calm tone. "Look, when Tiffany was a baby, Aimee wouldn't let me take her anywhere, and I understood that. I didn't know anything about taking care of an infant. And as she grew, Tiffany didn't know me very well. Of course she wouldn't want to go anywhere with a stranger."

"You're not a stranger. You're her father."

Jason acknowledged that with a nod. "But Aimee would just as soon I don't come around. She says it confuses Tiffany to have two fathers. When she's older—"

Kelli planted her hands on his desk and leaned over it until her face was a foot away from his. "When she's older and realizes that her real father was too busy to be bothered with her, it's going to hurt her more than you can possibly imagine."

"She has a stepfather, and he's good to her." Jason hid a wince. It was a poor justification, and he hated the fact that he'd said it.

Curls flew with violence as Kelli shook her head. "I had Nana, and she was amazing. It doesn't matter. She needs to know she's a priority in her real father's life. That she's more important than a bunch of stupid zoo animals."

Anger stirred in Jason. Kelli's position was understandable, given her background, but this was Tiffany he was talking about. "Don't put me in the place of your parents, Kelli. That's not fair.

Besides, you're just as much a workaholic as I am. You're holding down two jobs, for goodness' sake, working all day and all night, too."

"Don't try to turn this around," she snapped. "We're not talking about me."

"Aren't we?" Jason stood and mimicked Kelli's posture with his hands on the desk, his face inches from hers. "I think you're putting me in your mother's place, and yourself in Tiffany's." He lowered his voice and held her gaze with his. "Don't do that, Kelli. This situation is totally different."

She sucked in a breath, preparing to speak. Jason braced himself for another verbal barb, but in the next second she closed her mouth. Her anger drained, leaving her eyes dark with a deep sadness that sent an answering twist to his chest.

"I'm sorry, Jason." Her whisper was almost inaudible. She backed away from him, shaking her head. "I can't do this."

As he watched her go, his limbs grew heavy. He dropped into his chair, unable to shake the feeling that even though she might stay around for the rest of her six-month obligation, Kelli had just disappeared from his life forever. And she'd taken his last chance at happiness with her.

Was she right? Were his motives selfish? Was he taking the easy way out by bowing to Aimee's wishes? Would Tiffany one day end up with the same pain hovering in her eyes that he'd seen in Kelli's every time Lil's name was mentioned?

He rocked backward in his chair. "Lord," he whispered, "You know I love Tiffany. I wouldn't hurt her for anything in the world. Maybe I ought to insist on spending time with her, whether Aimee likes it or not. Could You help me figure out what to do here?"

He didn't have the nerve to voice his final request, because he had no faith that even God could override the finality in Kelli's parting words.

Chapter Twenty-Three

"Gasira, target."

Raul issued the command in his gravelly voice while holding a tennis ball up to the porcupine's chain-link gate. The female porcupine obediently rose up on her back legs to press her nose against the fuzzy green ball, exposing her underside to her onlookers, just as the lion had done while Kelli watched earlier in the week. The exercise was completely unnecessary, in Kelli's opinion, because Gasira and Baya were so friendly anyway. But everything was being done today for the benefit of the trio of inspectors walking through the zoo with clipboards and sharp eyes that noticed everything.

"Good girl," Raul growled and thrust a carrot chunk through the gate. Gasira grabbed the treat, dropped to all fours and turned her quills toward her mate to protect it as she ate.

"Fine, fine," said the female inspector, whose name Kelli had forgotten five seconds after being told it.

Jason, who was accompanying the officials on their rounds, smiled his approval at Raul. Kelli kept her eyes on the porcupines, determined to ignore her boss unless she absolutely couldn't help it. But she couldn't seem to stop herself from watching him in her peripheral vision. And she couldn't stop the elated thrill she felt every time she was in his vicinity.

Cliff Reiker, the inspector whose name Kelli was unlikely to ever forget, made a quick note on his clipboard. "Next, I'd like to see a demonstration of the shift procedures with the western spotted skunk."

"Of course." Kelli had to hand it to Jason for keeping his voice completely even. "Raul, if you'll—"

"No." Reiker interrupted with a meaningful glance in Kelli's direction. "If you don't mind, I'd like to see her demonstrate the procedure."

Heat burned in Kelli's face as every eye turned her way.

"Uh, Kelli is officially still an assistant keeper," Jason explained.

Raul threw up a hand to stop him from refusing Reiker's request. "She can handle it."

Confidence flooded his tone. Raul had seen this coming and made her practice shifting Felix over and over since she returned from Denver. Even so, the little skunk was still nervous around her and only cooperated about half the time. Battling nerves that fluttered in her belly, Kelli led the small troop through the building to the skunk exhibit, dodging children and parents along the way. The inspectors took up positions outside the glass, their bodies angled so they could see the panel inside. Raul pressed a small handful of chopped yams into her palm, and she grinned her thanks. Felix adored yams.

Her fingers trembled as she unlocked the access door. She tried not to think about the last time Reiker had been here and what he might do if she failed so miserably this time. As she slipped inside, Jason shifted his position, his gaze fixed on her. Before she could stop herself, she glanced at his face. He caught her eye, smiled and gave her a private wink that sent an answering tickle to her stomach. Later on she might be angry with herself for the rush of giddy pleasure that wink caused, but right now she took comfort in the boost to her confidence.

Inside the closet, she was surrounded by darkness. At least she remembered to shut the door this time; she hoped Reiker noticed. The small crate Felix shifted into was outlined in the dark, and she picked it up before opening the panel. Light sliced through the darkness. On the other side of the glass, five faces watched as she blinked and scanned the enclosure. Felix had run beneath the hollowed log that served as his den, his pointy nose twitching in her direction as he watched her cautiously.

"Hey, Felix." She pitched her voice low and even added a little gravel so she sounded a bit more like Raul. "Don't be nervous."

She set the small crate inside the enclosure, directly in front of Felix's log, and opened her hand so he could see the goodies she held. "Look what I have here. Yum, yum. Your favorite snack."

With a toss, she placed the yams inside the crate. "Do me a favor, would you, buddy? Go on in. I promise you can come right back out again."

Her breath caught in her chest, Kelli backed away. For a moment that seemed to stretch into hours, Felix did nothing. Then he inched out of his hiding place, nose twitching, shiny black eyes darting from her to the food. With a lurch, he scampered inside the crate. Through the opening in the side, Kelli saw him pick up a piece of yam and begin to eat. Heaving a huge sigh, she closed the crate's metal door and latched it shut before glancing at her audience. All three inspectors were busy writing on their clipboards, but Jason and Raul both beamed at her. Raul shielded his hand with his body to give her a private thumbs-up.

She picked up the crate and peered through the side opening. "You were awesome, Felix. Good job."

Then she set the crate back down, let the skunk out, and when Felix had returned to his den with the last piece of yam held firmly in his teeth, closed and locked the access panel.

Outside, Cliff Reiker greeted her with a wide smile. "Nice work, Ms. Jackson."

Relief wilted her tense muscles. "Thank you."

She ignored Jason's smile of congratulations, but acknowledged Raul's grunt of approval with a grin.

The female inspector slid her pen beneath the clip on her board and dropped it to her side. "All right, that about does it. Unless either of you have something else you'd like to take a look at?"

Both men shook their heads. The group headed toward the exit, Kelli and Raul trailing behind them. Reiker hung back when the other two stepped outside. His gaze slid from Kelli to Jason.

"Everything looks good. I, uh, hope you understand that I had to report that incident." He sounded almost apologetic.

"We understood." Jason answered with confidence. "We weren't concerned."

"Good. You've got a great zoo here." He nodded goodbye and followed his fellow inspectors outside.

Jason hung back. Kelli felt his gaze on her face, but she didn't look at him. Instead, she watched the squirrel monkeys perform acrobatics on their tree in the nearest exhibit.

"Are you scheduled to work the weekend?" he asked Raul.

"Why?" Raul asked, eyes narrowed.

Jason lifted a shoulder. "I'm taking a couple of days off. Just wanted to make sure we've got all the bases covered."

Raul grunted. "I'll be here." He jerked a head toward Kelli. "Her, too."

Jason nodded. "All right. I'll see you Monday, then."

He disappeared through the door without another look in Kelli's direction. When he'd gone, Raul stared after him.

"Can't remember the last time that boy took a day off," he muttered. Then he noticed Kelli. "You're done here," he told her gruffly and waved a hand in the direction Jason had gone. "Go help somebody else." He peered at her from beneath his scraggly eyebrows. "But come back in the morning."

She sketched a mock salute. "Aye-aye, sir."

Outside in the sunshine, Kelli sidestepped around a pair of laughing girls on their way into the building. The triumph of her victory with Felix was starting to wear off, and the lingering sense of emptiness she'd battled for two days threatened to return. She glanced at her watch. Four-thirty. In another half hour she could leave, arrive at Barb's house in time to chat with Nana as she ate dinner in bed, and then head home to spend yet another night alone with the cat, working on her clients' accounts. In the morning she'd get out of bed and follow exactly the same routine as today.

What is Jason doing this weekend?

The thought made her feet move faster, as though she could run away from the nagging sense of loss she felt every time he came to mind. It wouldn't work; it never did. Still, she found herself speed-walking over the well-groomed pathways until she came to a halt at the place she found herself returning to over and over—the orangutan exhibit.

Cocoa was napping on her platform. Kelli waited until the family in the observation area left, then stepped up to the wall. She folded her hands and rested her arms on top of the concrete, and watched the slumbering ape. Jason's words, uttered the last time she'd stood here with him, played over and over in her mind.

Is he right? Am I becoming bitter because I can't forgive my mother for abandoning me?

Far below, water trickled in Cocoa's moat. Childish laughter drifted to her from somewhere in the distance. Neither sound was enough to drown out her thoughts.

"I don't want to be bitter, Lord," she whispered. "But forgiving her is like excusing what she did, like saying it didn't matter. And it *does* matter."

Cocoa stirred on her platform. She rolled over, cast a glance in Kelli's direction and then turned away again without performing any of her usual antics. Kelli smiled in spite of herself. Apparently an audience of one wasn't enough to interrupt her nap. Kelli had grown fond of the orang since watching her enjoy the yellow piñata. She certainly was a crowd-pleaser, an important attribute for a zoo animal.

What had happened to the baby orang? Had he grown up happy and healthy with his foster mother, as Kelli had with Nana?

"Stop it," she scolded herself. "I'm not an animal, and neither was my mother."

If only Lillian had told her about the cancer last January, Kelli could have done something.

Like what? Would I have taken a leave of absence from my job to take care of her?

She leaned forward over the wall and peered at Cocoa's sleeping form as she weighed her thoughts. Yes, she would have. Because that way, she could have cleared the air between them. She would have given Lillian a chance to explain, to apologize. And she would have forgiven her before it was too late

But is it too late now? Isn't this whole six-month condition Lillian's way of making peace between us? Isn't the lesson of Cocoa her way of trying to explain, to ask forgiveness?

Like her mother, Cocoa was a disaster at motherhood. But she was a great orangutan. And Jason had said one day they would try again to introduce her to another orang. She would be given another chance.

Everyone deserved another chance, didn't they?

Lillian did mention forgiveness at the end, in her final letter. What was it she said? "I hope God forgives me. I don't expect you to."

And why would she? In the past several years, Kelli complained angrily to Nana about Lillian's infrequent phone calls, but had she ever once initiated a call herself? Tears blurred her vision. She dropped her head onto her arms and closed her eyes. Jason was right. She'd grown so bitter that her own mother died alone because she didn't think Kelli cared.

Hot tears escaped her clenched lids and traced a trail down her nose. "I'm sorry, Mom. I forgive you. I hope you'll forgive me, too."

Her tears fell unchecked, accompanied by quiet sobs from the dark recesses of her soul. When the last tear splashed into Cocoa's moat far below, the bitterness that had weighed her down disappeared with it.

Chapter Twenty-Four

"Look, Daddy! A whole bunch of monkeys!"

Excitement pitched Tiffany's little-girl voice even higher than normal. At the sound of his daughter calling him *Daddy,* Jason couldn't keep a goofy, proud smile off his face.

"They're called howler monkeys." He allowed her to pull him by the hand toward the exhibit. "Want to know why?"

She ran up to the iron railing, stepped up on the bottom rail, and dropped his hand to dangle her arms over the top. "Yeah. Why?"

"Well, when they—" He didn't have to continue, because at that moment one of the howlers provided a live demonstration.

Tiffany clapped delicate hands over her ears and turned a wide-eyed face up toward him. "Ouch! They're loud! Daddy, let's run away."

She grabbed for his hand, and the two of them ran from the howler exhibit, Tiffany's happy giggles filling his ears. Jason couldn't keep his eyes off of his beautiful daughter. Her brown curls, a shade more golden than his, bounced whenever she moved, and her dark eyes sparkled with interest in everything she encountered. She was one of the most outgoing children he'd ever seen, eager to meet new people despite Aimee's dire prediction of extreme shyness and fear. And, of course, if his heart wasn't already captivated when she squealed with excitement at the prospect of spending the whole day with him, he was putty in her hands when she actually *asked* to go see the zoo where he worked.

Tiffany slowed to a skip, her hand still clutching his. Jason didn't quite skip across the paved trail, but he stepped with a bounce that might possibly pass for one.

"Ooh, look at that, Daddy!" Tiffany pointed ahead. "It's a bear."

Jason tore his eyes away from his daughter to look where she pointed. Two zoo employees approached from the direction of the bear exhibit. Sherry and—his pulse stuttered when he identified the second.

Jason stopped in front of them.

"Well, hello there." Sherry wore a wide smile. "And who do we have here?"

"This is my daughter, Tiffany." He spoke to Tiffany, but his gaze was fixed on Kelli's stunned face. "Tiff, this is Miss Sherry and Miss Kelli. They work at the zoo, too."

Kelli mastered her surprise and a smile transformed her expression. She stooped down to put herself on eye-level with the child. "Hello, Tiffany. It's nice to meet you. Are you having a fun day with your dad?"

Curls bounced as Tiff nodded. "My daddy is the boss of this whole zoo." Her expression became serious. "Is he your boss?"

Kelli grinned. "Yes, he is."

The little girl turned a knowing smile up at him. "I thought so."

Sound erupted from the radio on Sherry's belt. "We have a code blue with Samson. Repeat, code blue with Samson. Pete's on the way."

The blood in Jason's veins turned to ice. Samson! Something had happened to the lion. Sherry whirled and ran in the direction of Samson's cage. In the same moment, Jason swooped Tiffany into his arms.

"What is it?" Kelli asked. "What's a code blue?"

"Medical emergency," Jason called over his shoulder as he raced after Sherry.

He was vaguely aware that Kelli followed. He rounded a curve in the path and saw that a crowd had gathered around the lion exhibit. Tightening his grip on Tiff, he pushed his way through the people until he stood at the rail beside Sherry.

Samson prowled back and forth, a snarl rumbling through curled lips as he showed yellow fangs. The smooth-sided artificial tree had broken apart, and the top half lay on the concrete floor. Sharp-looking bolts protruded from the lower half. The cage furniture was old, but Jason didn't realize it was in danger of collapsing. Hadn't Michael been performing regular inspections?

When Samson reached the end of the enclosure, he turned, and the crowd gasped. Jason saw the reason for the code blue. The tawny golden fur was sticky with blood, which seeped from a deep wound in the lion's side. Those artificial trees easily weighed over a hundred pounds. Apparently a bolt had gashed into the flesh during the collapse.

"All right, we've got to clear this area," he told Sherry, then raised his voice and addressed the people around him. "The veterinarian is on the way. I'm afraid you'll all need to get back, out of the lion's sight. We need to keep him as calm as possible, and crowds will only make him more anxious."

Sherry began the process of herding the people backward. Jason realized Kelli stood behind him, her round eyes fixed on Samson. In a detached part of his mind, he recognized that her presence was an act of bravery on her part, but he'd praise her for that later. Right now, he needed her to work.

"Kelli, take Sherry's keys and run to the storage room behind the cougar exhibit. Set up orange cones on each end of this path to keep the people out." He used one hand to point at the areas where he wanted the barriers placed, the other still clutching Tiffany.

She jerked a nod and ran off to do as he asked.

"Where's Michael?" Jason asked Sherry.

"He called in sick today," she told him over her shoulder as she followed the crowd away, arms outstretched as though shooing chickens.

Terrific. We're short-handed again.

"Daddy, does the lion have a boo-boo?" Tiff's voice in his ear was sad.

"Yes, sweetie, he does. But the doctor's coming soon."

It seemed like hours before Pete zoomed up on a converted golf cart. By that time Kelli had erected the cone barriers, and every available keeper had arrived. Raul, Sherry, Erica, Cameron and Kelli clustered around him, awaiting instructions. Behind him, Samson's frantic pacing had increased. The angry snarl never stopped.

Pete extended his neck to see Samson's wound, climbed off the bench seat and went around to the rear of the cart where he unstrapped a long black case. He clicked it open and lifted out the tranquilizer gun. "All right, who's going in with me?" His voice was completely calm.

Almost as though he sensed what was coming, Samson chose that moment to lift his head and utter a ferocious roar. Kelli's eyes went even rounder with barely controlled panic and her gaze snapped to Jason's face.

Tiffany gave a squeak of fear and clutched his neck with both hands. "I'm afraid, Daddy."

Jason hugged her tight. "Shhh, sweetie. There's nothing to be afraid of. The lion is hurt, and the doctor's going to make him feel better."

She buried her face in the curve of his neck. "I want to go see the screaming monkeys again." A sob choked her voice.

For a single instant, Jason was torn. With Michael gone, he was the keeper with the most experience working with Samson.

He should be the one to accompany Pete into the enclosure and take care of the lion's injury.

But there was absolutely no choice involved. The little girl clutching his neck trembled with fear, and there was nothing in this world—not even Samson—that could pry her away from him.

He caught Kelli's eye as he spoke. "You'll have to handle it yourselves." Then he nuzzled his lips against Tiffany's ear. "Come on, sweetie. I have a great big monkey to show you."

"Okay, Daddy." Relief saturated the muffled voice.

As he walked away, he heard the keepers discussing who would assist Pete and who would work to clear out the broken cage furniture. Just before he turned the corner, he glanced backward. Kelli stood watching him leave, a battle of emotions raging on her face.

She thrust her chin forward and announced in a voice that carried across the distance, "I'll help Pete with the lion."

Chapter Twenty-Five

*K*elli's heart pounded so loud she couldn't hear anything else. Did she just volunteer to go into the cage and actually help the veterinarian treat a lion? She must have, because the others were already planning which of them would stay out to keep the crowds away and who would remove the broken logs. Jason's hundred-watt smile reached her across the distance in the instant before he disappeared around the corner with his daughter.

Thank You, Lord, that he took her away. If that lion wakes up while we're in there, I don't want her to see me get eaten.

Her mouth filled with cotton as she followed Pete to the corner of the cage. He thrust the end of the dart gun through the fencing, the other end secured against his shoulder. His bushy gray beard brushed his arm as he leaned his head down to take aim. Kelli held her breath as the lion turned.

Pete pulled the trigger. The dart zipped out of the barrel with a loud *Pppffftt*.

In the next instant, Samson's hindquarters jerked. He turned and rushed toward them, his ferocious roar going before him like a battering ram. Both Kelli and Pete jerked backward as he threw his body against the welded mesh. Fear made Kelli's head light, her breath fast and shallow. She couldn't get over the idea that the lion was glaring at her, memorizing her face so if he ever got the opportunity to repay her for this indignity, he knew who to come for.

"Perfect shot." Pete gave a satisfied nod. "Now we'll just wait."

The others circled around, every eye turned toward the lion. Kelli's pulse slowed almost imperceptibly as they watched, silently, for the tranquilizer to take effect. At a noise behind them, Sherry hopped over the barrier and ran to shoo away a pair of children who had ignored the orange cone barrier.

"We have to keep everything around him quiet." Pete's voice was low, his tone even. "No excitement. A rush of adrenaline will render the drug ineffective."

Kelli tried to swallow against a completely dry throat. She couldn't utter a sound if she'd tried.

Finally, Samson's pace slowed, and a few moments later, the big cat collapsed. Still, Pete insisted that they wait and even poked the lion with a long pole through the barrier to be sure he was completely out.

Satisfied, he stooped to pick up his medical bag. "We're ready."

No, we're not, Kelli wanted to scream, but she didn't dare. With every inch of her being she wanted to call Sherry, to insist on trading places. It made more sense for her to keep the public away and let someone who'd actually been trained to take care of animals assist Pete.

But a tiny flicker of determination held her back. If she ran away now, she would be stalked by terror for the rest of her life. She had to face her fear if she ever hoped to master it.

She would have prayed, but couldn't form a single coherent thought. Instead, she directed a wordless plea toward heaven, gathered what shreds of courage she could and followed Pete through the access panel.

The veterinarian rushed right over to Samson's side and knelt beside him. Erica and Cameron hurried toward the broken logs and began working to loosen the remaining bolts. Kelli had to force her feet to take each step across the concrete splattered with the lion's blood. Finally, she arrived at Pete's side and stood staring down at his patient.

Samson was impossibly, terrifyingly huge. His paws were easily the size of Kelli's head, his body at least six feet long, not counting the tail. A strip of dark fur decorated the back of the shaggy mane that covered his neck, head, and even formed a beard that made Pete's look scraggly. The fur beneath his nose and on his chin was white, just like Leo's.

Pete probed the wound with gentle fingers. "It's a deep wound. Probably extremely painful for the poor creature."

With a dawning sense of surprise, Kelli felt the stirrings of compassion. The regal face, eyes closed in drug-induced sleep, belonged to a helpless animal whose species was endangered. He depended on zoo employees to take care of him. Zoo employees just like her.

"We're in luck." Pete straightened from his examination of the wound. "It's deep, but there doesn't appear to be any internal damage. Kelli, would you open my bag and hand me the blue pouch you'll find in the inside pocket?"

Kelli did as she was told, working mechanically to assist Pete in administering an injection to numb the area of the injury and then suture it closed. Erica and Cameron finished uninstalling the broken tree and carried the heavy pieces from the cage. They pulled the door closed behind them. Kelli swallowed back a fresh surge of fear and focused on Pete's hands. When the last stitch had been tied off, he calmly set about examining the animal, feeling the bones in all four limbs, listening to his heart and lungs.

"I like to take advantage of every opportunity to conduct a thorough examination of my patients," he explained as he worked, "because they don't come along often. Hand me that syringe, please. He's lost a fair amount of blood, but he won't miss a bit more."

As Kelli reached for the syringe, a movement drew her eye. The tip of the lion's tail flicked upward.

"Uh, P—" Her voice choked off in her throat. She swallowed and tried again. "Pete. His tail's moving."

Pete's expression did not change as he uncapped the syringe. "Yes, it's about time for him to wake up."

An icy finger slid down Kelli's spine. "Then let's get out of here."

"In a minute."

Pete pressed his fingers along Samson's front leg for a moment, then plunged the needle in. The tail flopped, and this time the lion's lips moved upward into the first hint of a snarl. Blood roared in Kelli's ears.

"Pete!" Her whisper hissed.

He didn't answer, but slowly pulled the plunger outward. Red fluid filled the clear barrel as the lion's whiskers twitched. Kelli's head felt light. She couldn't take her eyes off that flickering tail. Every molecule of her body shouted *Hurry! Hurry!*, but the veterinarian, unfazed, refused to be rushed. He finished drawing blood, capped the needle and calmly slipped it into a protective case before storing it in his medical bag.

Kelli was on her feet, across the cage, and waiting by the door when he gave his ferocious patient an affectionate pat on the back. Finally, he joined Kelli and together they left the exhibit.

When the final door was closed and locked behind her, Kelli sank against it, drawing deep draughts of air into her lungs.

"Nice work, Kelli," Pete told her with a satisfied nod. "You can act as my assistant anytime."

Together with Sherry, Cameron and Erica, they moved around to the front of the lion exhibit and watched as Samson's movements increased. Within a few minutes, he was struggling to get to his feet. When he finally heaved himself upright with a groggy effort, a fierce wave of triumph flooded Kelli. She'd done it! She'd actually gone into the same enclosure with a lion, touched the creature, helped to heal its wounds. Her voice joined the others in a cheer.

Cameron unclipped the radio at his belt. "Code blue is over. Samson is fine."

Kelli's ears pricked up when Jason's voice answered. "Thank the Lord. Excellent work, everyone."

She grabbed the radio out of Cameron's hands. "Where are you?"

"We're at the snack bar. Come on over and I'll buy you an ice cream cone to celebrate."

Kelli handed the radio back to Cameron, unable to stop from beaming at the little group around her. "Anyone else going?"

Sly grins broke out on every face.

"Uh, I don't think his invitation was for everyone," Cameron told her.

Sherry wore a smirk as she shoved Kelli with an elbow. "Definitely not."

Even Pete seemed to be having a hard time hiding his smile as he patted her arm. "You go ahead, my girl. We'll wait and hear about it over the lunch table tomorrow."

The flush that warmed Kelli's face as she left them by the lion's exhibit might have been from the humid heat. Or maybe not.

The lunch crowd filled the umbrella-covered picnic tables that surrounded the snack bar. Kelli shielded her eyes and looked for Jason. A waving hand at the other side of the area snagged her gaze and drew it to Jason's wide grin. She returned his wave with one of her own, her pulse pounding a funny tempo as she threaded her way to him.

Jason stood waiting beside a table that bordered the playground equipment. What would she say to him? She'd behaved so badly in his office, shouting at him and accusing him of deserting his daughter. She needed to apologize, but as she drew near and looked up into his eyes, any words she might have uttered flew out of her mind.

Jason didn't speak either. Instead, he opened his arms and held them wide in a silent invitation. Wordlessly, Kelli stepped into his embrace. Her awkwardness faded away as his arms encircled her.

"You did it," he said. "You conquered your fear of lions."

"Well, I wouldn't say that." Her laughter was muffled against his shirt. "Don't expect me to volunteer to be Samson's keeper anytime soon."

His arms tightened as he whispered in her ear. "I'm so proud of you."

A warm thrill shot through her. "Thank you." She pulled back and looked at the half-eaten cheeseburger and plastic child's cup resting on the table. "Where's Tiffany?"

The proud smile that crept across Jason's lips sent a thrill of a different kind straight to her heart. He looked toward the playground equipment and called. "Hey, Tiff. Come say hi to Miss Kelli."

Kelli turned in time to see the beautiful little girl give a giant leap off the swing, land on her feet and run toward them without a pause. She screeched to a halt in front of Kelli and looked up at her through those familiar-shaped eyes.

"Hi, Miss Kelli."

"Hi, Tiffany. Are you having fun?"

The child nodded as she picked up the cheeseburger, took a giant bite and tossed it back on the table. Still chewing, she said to Jason, "Can I go play some more? Pleeeeeeease?"

Jason nodded. "Sure."

She ran off, shouting over her shoulder, "Watch me, Daddy. I can swing higher than anybody."

Laughing, Jason called after her, "Just be careful!" He grinned down at Kelli. "I don't even want to think about what her mother would do to me if I brought her home with a broken arm the very first time I took her out."

He dropped down onto the bench, his back to the table so he could keep an eye on the playground, and with a gesture invited Kelli to sit beside him. She did, pleased when he scooted close enough to drape an arm casually behind her.

"How did you manage to get permission to take her?"

A scowl twisted his profile. "I didn't ask. I called Aimee Wednesday night and told her I had a legal right to weekend visitations with my daughter, and if I had to get the court to enforce it, I would."

Wednesday night. That was the night they were supposed to go on their date. The day she'd shouted at him, accused him of not caring about his child.

Kelli folded her hands in her lap and stared at them. "I'm sorry for what I said, Jason. I shouldn't have spoken to you like I did."

He slid his hand between hers. "I needed someone to knock sense into my head. That's what friends are for." He entwined his fingers with hers. "Will you make me a promise?"

Depths opened in his eyes, and Kelli felt herself falling into them. Unable to speak, she nodded.

"Promise me you'll *always* feel free to tell me what you think."

The emphasis he gave the word held a wealth of possibilities. *Always* meant far longer than six months. And it was a promise between two people who were far more than friends.

Swallowing past a lump of emotion, Kelli nodded. "I promise."

Chapter Twenty-Six

"I love mashed potatoes." Tiffany stuffed a forkful into her mouth. She swallowed without chewing and then scowled at her plate. "I don't love broccoli."

Kelli laughed across the table at the child's expression. "I used to hate broccoli, too." She speared a bright green bite. "But this is good, especially with the sauce your grandma put on it."

Tiffany's scowl turned skeptical as she watched Kelli chew. "I don't love sauce either."

Seated in the chair next to her, Barb put an arm around the little girl and hugged. "If my granddaughter doesn't want to eat broccoli, she doesn't have to."

Tiffany beamed up at Grandma, while on the other side of her, Jason pulled an outraged face. "Is this the same mother who wouldn't let me leave the table until I finished everything on my plate?"

Barb reached over with a fork and scooped the offending vegetable onto a bread plate. "There. Now it's not on her plate."

They all laughed. Watching Barb dote over her granddaughter made so many lovely memories surface from Kelli's childhood. She exchanged a smile with Nana. The special bond between grandmothers and granddaughters was being reborn in this house tonight, right before their eyes.

But that was nothing compared to the other bonds that were being formed. When Jason looked at her across his mother's table, Kelli's heart swelled until she feared it would burst. Her mind sang the truth that resonated throughout her soul: *I'm in love with a zookeeper!*

Beside her, Nana's head sagged forward, and Kelli was instantly on her feet. "Nana, let me help you back to your room."

"I haven't finished my dinner." But the protest sounded weak.

"I'll bring your plate, and you can finish in bed," Kelli promised.

Jason left the table to retrieve the walker and placed it within reach of Nana's chair. "You've been out of bed for an hour already, and that's the longest time since you got home from the hospital."

"I do feel a little tired."

Nana allowed Jason to help her out of the chair, and Kelli walked beside her as she inched, wincing, toward the door.

When they passed the chair where Tiffany was seated, the little girl leaped out of it. "I'll give you a goodnight kiss."

For an instant, Kelli feared the lively child would knock Nana off her unsteady feet. But when she approached the walker, she calmed and rose onto her tiptoes. Jason lifted her up to place a gentle kiss on Nana's wrinkled cheek.

A weary smile hovered around Nana's lips. "Good night, honey. I hope you visit again soon."

"I will, Nana," the little girl promised in her childish voice.

As Kelli assisted Nana toward the door, Jason helped Tiffany climb back into her seat.

"Daddy, is Nana my grandma, too?" she asked as Jason scooted her chair close to the table.

Jason caught Kelli's gaze over the child's head. A slow, dizzying smile brightened his face. "Not yet, sweetie."

The love shining in his eyes made Kelli's heart sprout wings and soar.

Epilogue

Three Years Later

*F*olding chairs lined the viewing deck, most of them occupied despite the humid Florida heat, and still people crowded into the area. Kelli stood near the iron rail on one side, watching as her mother-in-law helped Nana into the seat that had been reserved for her on the front row. Barb got Nana seated and then slid into the chair next to her.

"Daddy, let me hold him. It's my turn."

Kelli turned a smile on seven-year-old Tiffany, a bright picture of beauty in her yellow sundress and curly pigtails. She lifted her arms up toward her father.

"He's wiggly today, honey. He might squirm right out of your arms."

Jason clutched the baby tightly, as though he couldn't bear to give him up. Kelli knew how he felt. Her arms ached to grab six-month-old David Greg and cuddle his chubby neck until he squealed with laughter.

Tiffany eyed her baby brother, her busy mind trying to come up with a bargain her father would accept. "I'll sit down by Grandma. That way I won't drop him."

Jason turned a grin toward Kelli. "All right. But you have to promise to keep him quiet during the ceremony."

"No problem, Dad."

Tiff raced to the chair beside Barb, and Kelli watched as Jason settled their son in her lap. Then he returned to her side, a bemused expression on his face.

"She called me Dad." He shook his head. "Suddenly I feel like an old man."

Kelli laughed and rose on her toes to plant a kiss on her husband's cheek. *"Old Man* comes later, when she's a teenager."

Jason groaned.

A second of static came from the radio at his belt, followed by Michael's voice. "Samson's getting restless down here. How much longer is it going to be?"

Jason glanced at his watch and then into the gathering crowd. "I'm just waiting for the last of the—oh, there's Lewis now."

Kelli looked up and saw Mr. Lewis making his way through the press of people. On the second row, Francine Cowell waved to get his attention, and he made his way to the empty seat beside her. The entire board of directors had now arrived for the ceremony.

"We're starting now, Michael." Jason released the button on the radio and looked at her. "Are you ready?"

Nerves fluttered in her stomach as she scanned the crowd. Public speaking had never been her strong point. Of course, zookeeping wasn't her forte either, but in the three years since Lillian's death she'd gone from full-time accountant to full-time zookeeper. And then since little Davie's birth, to part-time keeper and full-time mom. If she could handle a cage full of hungry primates and a cranky baby, she could certainly give a speech in front of a crowd.

Jason stepped in front of her. She tilted her head back to look into his face, and when she did, he leaned down. His lips moved tenderly against hers, the kind of kiss she most loved from him.

He pulled away and whispered, "I love you. Knock 'em dead."

Her heart full, Kelli stepped to the center of the viewing deck, directly in front of the giant red ribbon they'd strung across the railing. She picked up the microphone they'd placed there earlier, faced the crowd and waited until everyone fell silent.

"I'd like to thank you all for coming today. As you know, Cougar Bay is committed to providing excellent care for its animals, and to becoming a leader in global wildlife conservation. We are proud that you, the visiting public, have caught our vision. Your generous contributions over the past three years have made this expansion project possible."

She paused to clear her throat. Her gaze fell on Nana, who watched with undisguised pride shining from her eyes.

"Though the expansion has been a combined effort, it started with one woman. My mother had a dream. She wanted to see an African Lion Habitat built at Cougar Bay."

Emotion threatened to squeeze her throat shut. She had gladly given up her goal of opening an accounting firm by donating part of her inheritance in order to see her mother's dream fulfilled. Kelli turned to let her gaze sweep over the lion habitat that lay behind her. A half-acre of land, surrounded by a wide moat and covered with protective mesh, sprawled in front of the new building. Sturdy trees cast deep shade over part of the enclosure, and gigantic boulders provided plenty of places to bask in the sunlight. The new building, a low concrete structure twice the size of the old lion cage, stood at the opposite end. Lillian's ashes had been scattered beneath the foundation, back when they'd broken ground on the building six months ago, so her earthly remains would sleep beneath her beloved lions.

She faced the crowd again. "My mother died three years ago. But due to a million-dollar grant from her estate, Cougar Bay was able to build this exhibit. So it is with deep pleasure that I have the honor of dedicating the Lillian Mitchell African Lion

Habitat. It will serve as a lasting monument to her memory and as a home to the animals she loved."

Jason stepped forward, a giant pair of ceremonial scissors in his hand. He placed the blades on the ribbon and waited for her to put her hands on the handles alongside his. At his nod, they cut the ribbon together. The crowd applauded.

Jason unclipped the radio. "Now, Michael."

A panel in the building slid upward. Tiffany jumped out of her seat, rushed forward to hand the baby to Kelli and stood beside her daddy to watch as the crowd pressed around them.

Samson exited the building slowly, caution apparent in every taut muscle of his body. He stopped just outside and lifted his head, blinking in the sunlight. For a moment he stood still, his head sweeping sideways as he examined his surroundings. Then he took a cautious step, testing the ground beneath his giant paws.

"Why doesn't he run?" Tiffany asked.

"He's just checking things out," Jason explained. "He's never been on grass before."

Kelli snuggled little Davie tight in her arms and watched as Samson make his first wary circuit of his new enclosure.

It's really happening, Lillian. Your dream is coming true.

Kelli looked up at her husband. He gave her the private grin that never failed to make her pulse skip, then put an arm around her and pulled her close to his side. Kelli snuggled into the familiar curve of his body, her heart full.

Mine has already come true.

QUESTIONS FOR DISCUSSION

1. Jason tells Kelli that animals have a kind of sixth sense to tell when someone doesn't like them, and they tend to avoid those people. Have you found that to be true?

2. Why does Kelli feel like she broadcasts signals that she's unlovable? What caused these feelings in her?

3. How did Jason's past mistake affect his relationship with others in his life?

4. Why has Jason chosen not to be an active part of Tiffany's life? Was he right in his choice?

5. Are the restrictions imposed by AZA on animal breeding in zoos beneficial? Why, or why not?

6. How did the traumatic experience Kelli suffered as a child affect her ability to form romantic relationships?

7. What were Lillian's reasons for the conditions of her trust? Was it cruel to force Kelli into a situation she had no desire to be in?

8. Jason and Kelli have vastly different opinions of Lillian. Which of them was correct?

9. Jason fears Kelli will become bitter if she doesn't forgive her mother. Is that true? How does Kelli finally find the ability to forgive?

10. When Kelli finds out about Tiffany, why is she so furious with Jason? Is her anger justified?

11. What part did Leo the cat play in helping Kelli overcome her fears?

12. Did you learn anything about zoo animals as you read *A Daughter's Legacy?*

13. Which was your favorite animal in this book?

BOOKS BY VIRGINIA SMITH

Mystery and Romantic Suspense
Murder by Mushroom
Bluegrass Peril
Into the Deep
A Deadly Game

Classical Trio Series
A Taste of Murder
Murder at Eagle Summit
Scent of Murder

Falsely Accused Series
Dangerous Impostor
Bullseye
Prime Suspect

Available through Annie's Book Club
Horse and Burglary
Triple Layer Treachery
Just Desserts
Thorn to Secrecy
To Hive and to Hold

Available from Guidepost Books
A Flame in the Night
The Last Drop of Oil

Contemporary and Romance
Lost Melody★
The Zookeeper's Daughter

Incredible Mayla Strong series
Just As I Am
Sincerely, Mayla

Sister-to-Sister Series
Stuck in the Middle
Age before Beauty
Third Time's a Charm

Historical Romance
The Heart's Frontier★
A Plain and Simple Heart★
A Cowboy at Heart★

A Bride for Noah★
Rainy Day Dreams★

★ co-authored with Lori Copeland

About Ginny

$\mathscr{V}$irginia Smith is the bestselling, award-winning author of nearly forty novels and a bunch of other stuff. She wrote her first story back in 1985 and submitted it to a magazine. It was promptly rejected. Thus began a long and painful lesson: writing well is a lot harder than it looks. Over the next twenty years she received 148 rejections, but finally managed to produce a piece of publishable fiction and in 2006 celebrated the release of her first novel, *Just As I Am*.

Known as Ginny to her friends, she loves Jesus, her family, writing, and geeking around on the computer, in that order. She also enjoys riding her motorcycle (a Triumph Bonneville T100 named Vickie) and scuba diving. And zoos. She loves zoos.

You can write to Ginny through the contact page on www. VirginiaSmith.org or, if you'd prefer to send a real letter, her mailing address is:

Virginia Smith
P.O. Box 4563
Frankfort, KY 40604-4563

Learn more about Ginny and her books at www.VirginiaSmith. org. She's on Instagram as @ginnypatricksmith. She occasionally manages to Tweet @VirginiaPSmith, or you can really get to know her on Facebook, where she spends far too much time. Facebook\ginny.p.smith.